IMPERIUM, INTERRUPTED – BOOK I

I0729387

ET TU, BRUTE?

JON SMITH

BAL
KON
media

ALSO BY JON SMITH

FICTION

The Fifth Horseman

Destiny Can Bite Me (Fang & Loathing #1)

The Stakeout Diaries (Fang & Loathing #2)

Rewrite the Dead (Fang & Loathing #3)

YOUNG ADULT

The Arb

CHILDREN'S FICTION

Toytopia

NON-FICTION

Once Upon A Brand

Founder Mode

The Bloke's Guide To Pregnancy

The Bloke's Guide To Babies

Get Into Bed With Google

Google Adwords That Work

Smarter Business Start-Ups

Start An Online Business

Digital Marketing For Businesses

ET TU, BRUTE
Published by Balkon Media

Paperback edition ISBN: 978-1-916970-13-7
Also available as an E-book

A CIP catalogue record for this title is available from the British Library.

Cover Design: Balkon Media

ONE

Decimus Flaccus had long ago determined that the truest measure of a man's character was not how he lived, but the degree of editorial intervention required to render his death presentable. This morning, he was wrestling with the career of Senator Rubellius—a man so undistinguished his name had to be checked twice each time it appeared in the records—who, according to the unredacted report, had expired in the privies behind the Subura's finest brothel. Decimus, hunched over his writing board in the scriptorium's coldest corner, regarded this fact with the grim serenity of a veteran undertaker. The death itself was neither unique nor, strictly speaking, a surprise, but it was his job to ensure Rubellius's passing would, when read aloud to the Senate, sound at least marginally less comedic.

He tapped the end of his quill against his front teeth, glancing between the uncensored dossier and his own draft. "Resolute virtue in the face of adversity" felt ambitious, even by the standards of funerary hyperbole. "Resolute" risked setting off sniggers among the junior tribunes; "virtue," deployed here, was nothing short of slander. He tried "unflappable dignity," then scratched it out before the ink dried. Finally, after a full minute spent re-reading the incident report's post-mortem footnote ("cause of death: catastrophic vascular event, seated"), he settled for "a steadfast servant of Rome, constant to the last."

The scriptorium—a word that in this instance meant the decaying west wing of the Curia Julia, third floor, next to the disused cloakroom—was alive with the sound of men attempting not to work. Dust clotted the air in slow motion. Every flat surface groaned under the weight of scrolls, folders, loose notes, and, in one corner, a petrified lump of cheese that had outlived the last three office-holders. The light came through cracked shutters in beams that illuminated nothing so much as the neglect. Somewhere nearby, a clerk coughed with the resolve of a man attempting to expel both lungs. Decimus ignored him.

He completed the final flourish on the draft, double underlined "exemplary" for no good reason, and began rolling the parchment into a neat tube. His hands moved with the precision of long practice, though the tip of his left forefinger bore the blue-black mark of a recent ink spill. He licked his lips, tasting the bitter tang of iron gall, and fished in his satchel for the official seal.

He was halfway through the act of melting a wax bead when the door burst inward on the smell of fish sauce and cheap soap. His supervisor, Marcus—known to the staff as "Marcus the Minor," not so much a comment on his age as on the supposed size of his ambition—swaggered into the room trailing the damp aura of an interrupted bath. He wore his toga as if he'd been forcibly wrapped in it while running, and his hair glistened with enough oil to lubricate a siege engine.

"Flaccus," said Marcus, without waiting for Decimus to look up, "your hand."

Decimus extended his right, palm up, which Marcus seized and shook twice, perhaps in a parody of camaraderie, perhaps to check for tremor. "Still attached," Decimus said, "and marginally more productive than the Senate as a whole."

Marcus produced a thin, predatory smile. "We have a priority request. Top tier. Straight from the Office of Civic Inspiration. The matter of Senator Rubellius is adjourned." He let go of Decimus's hand and immediately began to chew the skin around his thumbnail, leaving flecks of nail to drift down onto the papers below. "You are to redirect all effort to this. Immediately."

Decimus glanced at the document Marcus slapped onto his table. It was sealed in imperial red and tied with a gold thread. The header read: "Call for Historical Narratives – Consular Review, Year of Consecration." He suppressed a sigh. The only thing worse than composing eulogies was composing history for public morale.

"It's to be a stirring account of Caesar's rise," Marcus said. "For the masses. Not the actual masses, obviously.

For internal morale purposes. But it must read as though it could stir the actual masses. If the actual masses could read. Which they cannot, and let us pray, never do."

"Is there a deadline?" asked Decimus, but he already knew the answer.

"Yesterday," said Marcus. "But I've told them you're the best, so it'll be fine." He punctuated this with a swift glance at the door, as if expecting pursuit.

Decimus unrolled the new brief and read the instructions, which bore the unmistakable stylistic fingerprint of the Office's current secretary: "INSPIRING, IMPERIAL, LIGHT ON BLOODSHED." The final phrase had been underlined twice, which in Decimus's experience meant either a) the real story was a massacre, or b) the writer had recently witnessed one.

He nodded and began to tidy away Rubellius's file, pausing only to pencil in a note to himself—"double-check date of brothel collapse; possible metaphor for decline of state?"—before placing it in the overflow tray. The tray, like its owner, had ceased to overflow several years ago, but the label had not been changed.

Marcus lingered, his fingers now working at the wax on a nearby tablet. "One other thing," he said, lowering his voice. "The draft must include the recommended five omens, with at least two from avian sources. If you're short, invent them. But make it plausible. Not like last year's—'A pig was born with a senator's face.' Half the office lost their lunch." He coughed, and Decimus suspected he had been among them.

"Will there be an official review, or just the usual rubber-stamping by the augurs?" Decimus asked.

"Rumour is the augur in charge is that woman, Licinia," Marcus said, frowning as if the name itself tasted sour. "You know the one. Used to predict actual disasters, now reduced to approving poultry entrails." He shrugged. "I trust you'll find a way."

Decimus inclined his head, which was as close to a salute as he allowed himself in the presence of authority.

Marcus paused at the door, twisting back to add: "And do avoid metaphors about the state collapsing in latrines. Some of us have to read these aloud."

When he was gone, Decimus allowed himself a rare moment of exasperation, flicking a blob of ink at the wall. It joined an existing constellation of stains, forming what he privately called "the birth of Venus." He cleared a space on his desk for the new commission and set to work, gathering sources from the piles and unsealing a fresh bundle of waxed reports.

He was so absorbed in composing a suitably inspirational opening—"There are men who bend to fortune, and men who force fortune to bend to them. Caesar belonged, undoubtedly, to the latter tribe"—that he failed to notice the smell of burning until a fist rapped the lintel.

The messenger was Crispus, a youth whose normal state alternated between abject terror and utter confusion, sometimes both. He entered with his tunic slightly scorched and the whites of his eyes showing all round, clutching a wooden box labelled in red: "EMERGENCY AQUEDUCT RENAMINGS."

"Senior Flaccus?" Crispus squeaked, as if afraid the box itself would contradict him.

"That's me," Decimus said, not looking up from his

parchment. "If it's more documents, you can stack them on the cheese."

Crispus hesitated, shifting his weight from foot to foot. "It's urgent," he said. "It says so, here." He proffered the box, which Decimus took with both hands. The bottom left a dark smudge on the desktop.

He cracked the lid and found, not the anticipated flood of plumbing complaints, but a battered packet of auguries, a half-written ode to Victory, and a scroll tied with a ribbon the colour of dried blood. The scroll bore no official seal. Instead, someone had written in large, frantic script:

THE IDES ARE COMING – PREPARE THE FOOTNOTES

He lifted it out, turned it over. The reverse was blank except for the faint impression of someone having written, then erased, the phrase "Don't trust the birds."

Decimus squinted at the scroll, then at Crispus. "This was in the emergency aqueduct box?"

"Yes, Senior. It was at the top. The rest is just, um, pipes. And one complaint about a statue."

"Who brought it?"

"Someone from the Temple of Mars. They said it was a mix-up. Also, that the omens are not to be taken literally. They kept repeating that part."

"And the note?"

Crispus shuffled closer and whispered, "They said the augurs have been getting... threats. That they're not official. They said, 'If anyone asks, it's poetry.'"

Decimus eyed the handwriting again. He had seen worse verse.

He set aside the auguries and the ode, and unrolled the threatening scroll. It was indeed poetry, of a kind:

When crimson ties the Roman sky
And fowl unfit for augury
Refuse the knife and fail to die
Let writers mark the Ides to be

He closed the scroll, folded it neatly, and placed it atop the new assignment. For the first time in a week, he smiled—there was, at least, a sense of professional kinship. He considered tossing the note into the basket for "unsanctioned omens," but something in the meter appealed to him. He slid it into his satchel instead, next to his lunch.

Crispus lingered, peering at the remaining paper-work. "Is it true, Senior, that omens can be faked?"

"Not faked," said Decimus, who was not by nature superstitious, "just misinterpreted. With sufficient conviction, misinterpretation becomes history."

Crispus nodded as if this was wisdom, not thinly veiled despair, and retreated toward the door. Halfway out, he turned. "If you do need more birds, I can ask at the market. My uncle sells quail."

"I'll bear it in mind," said Decimus, already writing the heading for Caesar's biography. "And Crispus—next time, bring some cheese."

He worked through the noon hour, the din of the Curia fading as lunch drew the staff away. Left alone, Decimus drafted and redrafted, every line a compromise between the demands of history and the realities of audience. He avoided the bloodier details—Brutus's stunt with the roasted oxen, the incident with the cymbal player—though he left in a fleeting mention of the time Caesar singlehandedly talked down a drunken cohort by quoting Homer, mostly because Decimus admired the nerve.

The sun had shifted across the window by the time he reached the closing paragraph. The phrase "eternal Rome" felt both overused and insufficient, but he let it stand. He added a final, unrequested couplet, in the hope it might pass through unremarked:

And so the fates, with restless hand,
Entwine the stories of their land.

He leaned back, knuckles popping, and stared at the wall. The stain above his desk had, over the course of the day, taken on the distinct profile of Senator Rubellius. He was tempted to annotate it.

He gathered his drafts into a neat stack and prepared to deliver them for review, pausing only to check that the threatening note was still in his satchel. He could not have said why, but it seemed prudent to keep it close. Perhaps he feared some future historian would otherwise attribute it to Marcus.

As he walked out into the corridor, he found Marcus already waiting, hands clasped behind his back, eyes fixed on a passing cleaning woman. "Is it done?"

"Done enough for government work," Decimus replied.

"Splendid," said Marcus, taking the packet and tucking it beneath his arm with all the delicacy of a man carrying a dead cat. "They say the Ides will be unusually exciting this year. Best keep your head down."

"I intend to," Decimus said. But as Marcus slithered

off, Decimus found himself glancing at the blood-red ribbon in his satchel, and wondering whether, just this once, he ought to write his own footnotes.

By the sixth hour the sun had forced even the most shameless officials out of the Forum's glare, leaving only the marble statues and their pigeons to endure the city's light. Decimus, having judged his day's labours both substantial and insubstantial enough for a proper interval, picked his way across the fractured paving stones to a bench that, according to local legend, had supported the buttocks of every praetor since the Republic's invention. He sat, unwrapping his lunch and thoughts with equal reticence.

The so-called Bench of Moderate Triumphs commanded a view of the minor shrine to Obsequious Victory—a structure erected in the previous century to commemorate some campaign or other which no one presently recalled. The shrine was, like its subject, modest in both ambition and outcome. Its cornices sagged. The votive lamps smoked even when unlit. On its plinth, a now-faceless Victory gestured limply at the street.

Decimus chewed his ration of bread, which might once have been fresh during Sulla's dictatorship, and uncorked a tiny amphora of vinegar-spiked olives. He set about redacting a scroll of citizen complaints, a task that could be performed one-handed and had, on occasion, been attempted no-handed by cleverer scribes. The day's batch included a man furious about the price of lentils, a woman who claimed to have been menaced by "the same persistent donkey for three years," and a note in childish script complaining that "the water in the Tiber is all pee."

He struck through the more actionable allegations with a series of brisk diagonal lines, leaving only the blandest, most harmless laments for potential escalation. It was a point of pride that none of his redacted scrolls had ever provoked a riot.

Above, pigeons circled the shrine with the coordination of a drunken cohort, occasionally strafing the steps below. Decimus suspected they had grown more belligerent of late, perhaps in response to the poor quality of breadcrumbs on offer, or to the ambient mood of the city. He had once read that birds could sense civil unrest before men ever dared speak of it. He wondered if the same was true of bureaucrats.

From the Rostra, an amplified voice began to recite the hour's Senate decrees. It was, as usual, a litany of fiscal adjustments and statue removals. Decimus listened with half an ear:

"...the relocation of public urinals from the Via Sacra to the Circus Maximus is postponed pending further study of drainage patterns..."

Decimus rolled his eyes, and set his stylus down. The Forum was emptying. In the shadow of the Curia, he saw a cleaning woman drag a broken broom after her, pausing only to spit at a passing lawyer. He envied her candour.

A shadow fell across the bench. Decimus glanced up, expecting another crier, but found instead Hortensius, the city's most famously disgraced archivist. The man had aged in increments since his expulsion; his nose now drooped in sympathy with his jowls, and his toga—immaculate in the old days—was spattered with what might have been ink or, more likely, defeat. He sat beside Decimus without invitation.

"Redacting," said Hortensius, with a sniff that implied only an idiot would bother. "You know it's all copied anyway, don't you? Every 'private' scroll in Rome ends up in the City Record. They say there's a room under the Temple of Saturn filled with nothing but dupli-cate complaints. And in that room, another room, and so on, like a nest of rats eating each other."

Decimus offered him an olive, which Hortensius refused with a shudder. "If the duplicating rooms ever intersect," Decimus said, "will they cancel out? Or will Rome collapse under the weight of redundant grievances?"

"Redundancy is Rome's greatest product," said Hort-ensius. He produced from within his toga a battered flask and took a cautious sip, before smacking his lips with the satisfaction of a man who had known worse poisons. "You look tired, Flaccus."

"I am tired," said Decimus. "Of omens, and rewrites, and supervisors who cannot find their own elbows. Also, of bread." He broke off a piece and threw it to the pigeons, who descended as one with the fury of tiny glad-iators. "And yourself?"

"I exist," said Hortensius, which in the language of former chief archivists meant: I am plotting my revenge but need someone else to do the paperwork.

They sat in silence, watching the pigeons bicker over the bread. Hortensius broke first.

"Have you heard from the Office of Official Histories lately?" he asked. "They say you're writing the new Caesar. From scratch."

"Not from scratch. From a very selective collection of anecdotes," said Decimus. "With an inspirational motif and five omens, at least two avian. You can tell it's urgent because they delivered the brief in person. Along with a threatening poem."

Hortensius raised a sparse eyebrow. "The Ides are coming?"

"Very nearly." Decimus shrugged. "The warning is generic, but the meter is serviceable. I've kept it, in case the Ides take requests."

Hortensius gave a bitter chuckle. "It's a message. Someone wants to be found out." He leaned in, voice lowering. "When I was at the Temple of Apollo, I came across a scroll. Top shelf, back row, sealed in red. It was labelled PROPHECY—NOT FOR CIRCULATION. Naturally, I read it. Three days later, the augur who wrote it was found in the Tiber, headless. The scroll vanished, but copies circulated, of course. No secret stays secret in this city, not for long."

Decimus eyed him sidelong. "What did it say?"

"Does it matter?" said Hortensius, picking at the seam of his sleeve. "In Rome, the future is always the same: someone is murdered, and everyone else rewrites the reason why."

Decimus shifted, uncomfortable with the direction of the conversation. "If you've come to warn me, Hortensius, you should know I have no ambition worth assassinating. And I am not especially attached to my head."

Hortensius stared at him, eyes rheumy but oddly bright. "Ambition is not the point. Proximity is. Stand close enough to history, and you end up written into it whether you like it or not. Especially if you write footnotes."

Decimus watched the shrine, where a very old priest was lighting incense for an offering that no one else would witness. "I keep my head down," he said. "I write what they tell me. I don't add anything unless I must."

"That's your problem," said Hortensius. "You think omission is safe. It isn't. When the time comes, they'll come for the editors first. No one fears a poet. Everyone fears the man who redacts."

The pigeons, having finished their bread, resumed their patrol above the shrine. One landed beside Decimus's foot, regarding him with insolent red eyes. He nudged it gently with his sandal. It refused to move.

A street performer appeared in the square, accompanied by a lyre and a small audience of the very young and the very drunk. She launched into a song about Caesar's bald spot, each verse more ribald than the last. Around the Forum, heads turned in every direction except toward the sound. Decimus watched as the cleaner paused her sweeping to listen, then snorted and went back to work.

Farther off, near the public fountain, he saw the laundress Domitia wringing bloodstains from a toga with a violence that suggested the garment had personally offended her. Beside her, a youth in a trainee's sash appeared to be arguing the finer points of lye versus vinegar. The pair laughed, then resumed their respective tasks with renewed spite.

On the opposite end of the square, a tall woman with wild silver hair was engaged in animated conversation with a goat. Decimus blinked, realized it was Licinia, and was not especially surprised to see her so occupied. She released the animal, which bolted into the open, trailing bits of ribbon and sacrificial dye, and vanished up the steps of the Curia. Licinia herself stood for a moment, head cocked as if listening to instructions from above, then hurried after the goat, her robes flapping like a pennant in high wind.

Hortensius followed Decimus's gaze and smiled thinly. "The city endures. Always has. We're the only thing that changes, and never for the better."

He corked his flask, stood with effort, and regarded Decimus as one might a promising but doomed apprentice. "A word of advice," he said. "Write the story they want. Stay out of the footnotes. That's where the bodies pile up."

Decimus nodded, already knowing he would not follow the advice.

He watched as Hortensius shuffled away, then gathered up his redactions and olive stones, stowing them in his satchel with the day's other misgivings. He unfolded the threatening poem and read it again. This time he did not correct the meter. Instead, he returned it, unaltered, to his private folder—the one he would never admit to keeping.

Above, the pigeons resumed their slow, indifferent orbit. The old priest finished his incense and sat with his back to the shrine, gazing into the sun as if daring it to set. Decimus lingered on the bench until the shadow of the Curia finally overtook him, then rose to return to the scriptorium, where the duplicating rooms waited, and the future, as ever, required another rewrite.

TWO

The sun's afterbirth, that hour between dusk and true dark, found Decimus Flaccus winding through the Senate's lesser-known intestine: a corridor of such unyielding utility and aesthetic neglect it could only be loved by those who walked it daily. The walls sweated ancient damp behind flaking render, and the lamps—every third or fourth replaced with a cheaper grade—flickered in rhythm with the city's power struggles. The air was a broth of moulder, rat urine, and the philosophical notion of hope deferred. Decimus, alone but for his paperwork, savoured it as one might an old but honest wine.

He walked with eyes half-closed, so used was he to the uneven flagstones that he could have recited the sequence of dips and rises by touch. His mind, numbed by a day's worth of revised heroics, defaulted to compiling lists: metaphors for the latest water shortage, the hierarchy of acceptable eulogy synonyms, a tally of who owed him favours and who remembered. He scratched at a patch of dried ink on his wrist, noting with detached pride the density of the stain.

A hollow between two columns provided his habitual stopping point. Here, directly behind a brass wall-vent shaped like an eagle's beak, the Senate chamber's voices filtered through with a clarity unknown to those seated within. On previous evenings, Decimus had used the spot to gather material for anonymous satires—small, safe cruelties involving the flatulence of high office or the scandalous pigment choices of tribunes. Tonight, however, he intended only to jot a memo about the calcium residue clogging the western aqueduct.

He drew out his wax tablet, stylus in hand, and bent to the vent. The air stank of fish and men. Somewhere within, a meeting dragged on well past the agreed hour.

"…utterly unworkable," complained a voice, wet and plummy, "—the man is a menace, but we are not butchers."

A reply, razor-thin and knife-bright: "You prefer to be the butchered? Grow a spine, Marcellus. The calendar is on our side."

Decimus stiffened, stylus hovering. He recognised the first as belonging to Senator Marcellus—a man so renowned for his inaction that his colleagues described his career in terms of sedimentation. The second, though unnamed, had the intonation of someone who wrote his own press releases. Authority, unfiltered.

A scraping, as of cups or daggers or both. "We must be certain. The plan—"

"—is perfect if you can refrain from soiling yourself at the critical moment. The knives are arranged, the approach rehearsed. We even have an augur's silence, which is as good as blessing these days."

A pause. In the corridor, Decimus felt his pulse begin to imitate the unsteady lamps.

"But what if—" started Marcellus, then faltered.

The other voice: "There will be no prophecy, no omens. I have seen to it personally. All that remains is for you and the others to grow some testicles before the Ides."

Decimus, hand sweating around his stylus, pressed closer. He caught the quick shuffle of sandals as if one of the men had risen, perhaps to pace, perhaps to punctuate a threat.

"The Ides," repeated Marcellus, as if tasting the word for arsenic.

"It must be clean. History will do the rest. Leave the embellishment to our little friends in the scriptorium." The speaker gave a snort of contempt, an unlovely sound amplified by the vent's curvature.

Decimus's fingers, in their anxiety, snapped the stylus tip. The shattering noise echoed through the passage like a dropped sword. He scrambled to steady his tablet and instead lost control of his satchel, sending a small storm of scrolls, styluses, and lunch detritus cascading across the floor. In the confusion, a jar of inferior lamp oil toppled from its perch and rolled in slow-motion towards the far end of the corridor, trailed by an ooze of sticky resin.

Inside the chamber, the voices stopped.

Decimus's brain performed a full audit of his options and found that none were any good. Flight was impossible—the corridor's length offered no cover until the next intersection. Retreat was equally futile, the exit now distant and his satchel's contents marking a clear path of egress. He considered, briefly, dying where he stood, but concluded it would only add another statistic to the day's paperwork.

He ducked instead behind a monumental bust of Victory, headless since the Year of Cheap Chisels, and attempted to blend in with the other historical fragments. His heart thudded with such violence that he feared the entire Curia would hear it.

The vent, now silent, became a throatless witness to the moment. Decimus drew his knees up and fished, blindly, for his notes. His fingers closed around the red-threaded scroll—the "Ides" poem from the aqueduct box. The prescience of the thing sent a chill through him, or perhaps it was merely the corridor's air.

Footsteps approached the antechamber door. A hinge whined, and the blade of torchlight widened to reveal the silhouette of a man in full senatorial dress, the kind that only slightly disguised the lack of underlying manhood. Marcellus's head poked out, features lost in the glare, and scanned the length of the hall with the expression of a child expecting ghosts.

"Probably the scroll boy," he muttered, and shut the door with a soft, cowardly click.

From within, the second voice: "If he heard anything, he'll find himself posted to the Armenian border. Or a grave." A short, black laugh, then a return to low, urgent murmuring.

Decimus exhaled with such suddenness that he nearly fainted. He remained crouched behind Victory's truncated form until the voices faded and the lamps down the corridor began to dim in sequence—a signal, among the cleaning staff, that it was time to go home.

He gathered his scattered paperwork with trembling hands, sorting scroll from lunch by touch alone. He slipped the "Ides" warning into his sleeve and double-checked the vent, now choked with darkness. The stylus, snapped at the neck, he pocketed as a keepsake. He lingered another moment, testing each breath for signs of returning footsteps, then, satisfied, slunk back toward the scriptorium.

His gait was uneven, the dignity of public office mortally wounded. He ignored the janitor's raised eyebrow and the mosaic of his own footprints glistening in spilled oil. In the distance, the city's bells tolled the hour with the finality of a last rites.

In his satchel, the rhymed threat pressed against his ribs like a hot coal. He could not say what was more frightening: that a man might be killed in the Senate, or that it would be left to him to invent a reason for it.

At the mouth of the corridor, he paused, looked back, and memorised the pattern of shadows behind him. He would need the detail, later. As he stepped out into the night air, the wind caught and tore at the sweat on his face, and he realised for the first time that the day's true work had only begun.

The Office of Non-Urgent Citizen Grievances occupied an architectural blind spot of the Curia complex—a windowless chamber abutting the city wall, its only daylight a metaphysical one. The ceilings sagged from centuries of unresolved humidity, and the paint on the slogans had long since succumbed to the ambient despair: "JUSTICE EVENTUALLY," "YOUR VOICE, OUR FILING SYSTEM," and, for the motivationally inclined, "AT LEAST WE'RE NOT THE GALLIC OFFICE."

Here, the air was heavy with the industrial aftertaste of dried laurel leaves, a smell only amplified by the steady smoking of Clodia Scriba, Senior Intake Clerk and rumoured sole survivor of the Department of Honest Inquests. She sat at her desk with a posture that dared the world to improve, hair in a grey stubble, fingers yellowed and callused, eyes permanently narrowed from a decade of reading only the most joyless portions of the law. Her toga was the precise off-white of ancient bones, and her stamp pad glistened with the accumulated sweat of generations.

Decimus entered, clutching his battered folio, and immediately lost his nerve. The atmosphere was so perfectly engineered for emotional deflation that he found himself apologising for his own existence before he'd even reached the desk.

Clodia regarded him as one might a recurring fungal infection.

"State your grievance," she said, voice flat as a paving stone.

Decimus cleared his throat. He attempted, for the sake of dignity, to summon his best bureaucratic tone.

"Flaccus, Decimus. Office of Official Histories. I need to submit a VXL–4. Conspiracy, Treasonous, possibly Divine." He handed over the form, hands trembling only slightly.

Clodia took the parchment, barely glancing at the filled lines before sliding it into the "pending review" slot. Said slot was already in the process of slow combustion; a thin ribbon of smoke curled up the wall and joined a blackening patch near the ceiling. She reached for her stamp and marked the top corner "RECEIVED – PRIORITY: EVENTUAL" in a single, bored movement.

"Supplemental forms?" she asked, not looking up.

"Supplemental—?"

Clodia exhaled, sending a ghost of laurel vapour over the desktop. "Proof of Motive—Form 13C. Divine Approval, Omens Appendix 7. And at least one witness of reputable standing. Or goat."

Decimus attempted to swallow, found no moisture left, and instead produced a strangled squeak. "Surely the urgency—"

She cut him off with a flick of her stamp, which came down hard on the next form in the pile. "Urgency is not a category. Only 'immediate peril to Rome' bypasses standard procedure. You marked 'grave concern, time-sensitive,' which is two rungs below 'statue defacement' and only marginally above 'improper lustration'." She eyed him sidelong. "If you wish to escalate, you'll need to submit a Flavian Addendum, with accompanying hazard fee."

Decimus flinched. "I—"

She held up a finger, motioned for silence, then produced a sweetmeat from the depths of her desk drawer. She offered it in the way one might offer a treaty to barbarians.

He declined, and she shrugged, popping the confection into her own mouth. "Very well. I'll note your complaint. Is there a next-of-kin we should contact in the event of processing mishap?"

He tried to focus on the words, but his attention snagged on the fire, now eating its way through the pending tray at a methodical pace. "There's to be an attempt on Caesar. The Ides. It's not a rumour, it's—"

"Have you got the documentation?" She chewed slowly, each syllable measured and dispassionate.

"I—no. I mean, not yet. But I have a witness." He thought, desperately, of the cleaning woman and the janitor, but their value as witnesses hovered somewhere between zero and anecdotally amusing.

Clodia, unimpressed, reached for a new stack of forms. "Goat or better. Come back when you've got it." She stamped his complaint "Provisional: Pending Omen Clarification," the ink spreading into a perfect, damning ellipse.

Decimus felt his careful syntax unravelling. "You don't understand. They're going to do it. The omens—there's already a warning, it's circulating among the augurs, and—"

She stopped, finally looking at him with a flicker of genuine curiosity. "Omens, you say?"

He nodded, hope blurring reason. "A scroll, unsigned, alluding to the Ides. It reached my office disguised as aqueduct paperwork. The augurs are frightened. Or at least, they're pretending to be."

Clodia made a note, then drew out Omens Appendix 7 from the lowest drawer, dusted it off, and presented it with a flair that might have been irony. "Sign and date," she said. "If you can, have an augur initial here." She pointed to an impossible line, her nail yellow and blunt.

Decimus filled it in, hands shaking, and returned the sheet.

Clodia replaced the stack in its drawer, then, as if remembering a prior life, offered him another sweetmeat. This time he accepted, and it sat on his tongue, tasteless.

She regarded him for a moment. "Listen, Flaccus. They all come through here, sooner or later. The prophets, the lunatics, the senators with too much time and too little fibre. Most of it's noise. You want to make it stick, you need to play by the rules. Otherwise, it ends up here." She nodded toward the fire, now eating a new layer of grievances.

He stared at the flames, the perfectly bureaucratic self-immolation, and felt the futility settle on his shoulders like wet sand.

A commotion in the corridor. Crispus, tunic askew and hair smoking at the ends, burst into the office clutching a crate of confiscated augury birds and a divine tax exemption scroll. He looked first at Clodia, then at Decimus, then at the burning inbox.

"It winked at me," Crispus announced, producing a bloodied quail from the crate and holding it up like a sacred relic.

Clodia gave the bird a glance, then stamped a form "Misinterpretation – Class C" without breaking her rhythm.

Crispus, undeterred, dropped the bird on the desk, where it oozed something best left undescribed. He then turned to Decimus, eyes wide with either trauma or wine.

"They're saying the omens are all crossed. Nobody's reading them right. The augurs are fighting over the entrails. I heard two of them came to blows outside the baths."

Decimus wanted to laugh, or scream, or run until his legs stopped functioning. Instead, he thanked Crispus, picked up the quail, and dropped it gently into the wastebasket, where it landed atop a sheaf of unprocessed tax complaints.

He turned back to Clodia, who had already resumed her reading of the next petition.

"Is that all?" she said, not expecting an answer.

"Yes," said Decimus, and meant it.

He left the office, the echo of his sandals erased almost immediately by the sound of the stamp. Out in the corridor, he slumped against the wall, breathing in the familiar, exhausted air. From his satchel, the red-threaded scroll poked out, a reminder that some things, however urgent, would never be processed in time.

He considered, for a moment, the possibility of warning Caesar in person, but discarded it as both logistically and socially impossible. He was a historian, not a hero. The system would not save Caesar. The system, if anything, would footnote him.

He started back toward his own office, and wondered how the Ides would find him—surprised, or merely resigned.

The question, as with all things here, would be answered in triplicate, and not by him.

THREE

By midnight, the city's warmth had retreated into the walls, leaving the sub-basements of the Curia to the ghosts and their naturalists. Decimus Flaccus, not strictly one or the other, picked his way along the archive's lowest corridor, where the air changed from mildly unpleasant to actively suspicious. His sandals left damp prints on the flagstones, and his own breath, condensing in the chill, seemed to hover indecisively before dissolving. He had chosen the hour for its inhuman quiet. The old hands claimed this was when the records themselves whispered to each other, rehearsing the version of history that would survive until morning.

The entrance to the restricted stacks was less a door than a compromise, patched with whatever timber or scrap metal was to hand, and braced at the corners with twine thick enough to double as garrottes. Decimus paused, scanning the hall for witnesses—human or other-wise—then knocked twice, mimicking the rhythm of a dying heart.

The panel opened a thumb's width. A single, sleepless eye peered out.

"You're late," the eye hissed. "And you've tracked water over my manifest."

Decimus considered an apology, discarded it, and instead proffered a small, greasy packet. The eye glistened, then the door swung open to reveal Hortensius, the former Chief Archivist, now demoted to subhuman. He was clad in the same filthy robe, each stain a memory of former prestige. He seized the packet, tore it open, and snorted the contents (which proved to be a handful of illicitly imported poppy seeds) before shuffling aside.

The inside of the room looked like the last stand of an unpopular regime. Stacks of scrolls formed precarious ramparts, punctuated by jars of spent lamp oil and the remains of a thousand failed preservation techniques. Above it all hung the odour: mildew, desperation, and a sour tang of off-brand wine. The only light was a guttering lamp suspended from the ceiling by a ribbon of catalogue tags.

"Sit," commanded Hortensius, sweeping a pile of desiccated rat skulls off a crate. "But keep your mouth above the fungus line."

Decimus perched as directed, minding both the fungus and his own dignity. "I need information," he said, low and flat.

Hortensius grunted. "Everyone needs information. Most of them are satisfied with lies." He decanted a slug of wine into a cracked mug, then another into his own mouth. "Tell me the lie you'd like best."

Decimus set his elbows on his knees, hands locked to stop them trembling. "Is there a prophecy circulating? Something—anything—about the Ides?"

The archivist's smile was a slow-motion wound. "They don't send us the good stuff anymore. We're lucky if the gods bother to curse us with flatulence."

He finished the wine, wiped his mouth, and leaned in. "You didn't come for that. You have a scroll. Maybe two."

Decimus hesitated, then produced the red-threaded slip from his satchel. Hortensius's eyes flickered with a gambler's quick appraisal. "Handwriting's wrong for the official omens. Too much heart, not enough hedging. Was it anonymous?"

"Sort of," Decimus said. "It came via the aqueduct box. But the message is clear."

Hortensius unrolled the slip, squinted, then snorted. "That's not prophecy. That's a warning for people who still believe in consequences." He flicked the scroll back. "Have you taken it to the censors?"

"I tried." Decimus ran his thumb along the edge of the paper, resisting the urge to shred it. "They advised me to find a goat, or possibly a witness. I suspect the goat would be more forthcoming."

The archivist gave a laugh that was more exhalation than amusement. "You've come to the right place. If there's a goat behind this, I guarantee I've catalogued its droppings."

He reached under his seat, extracted a battered writing board, and began scribbling with a quill that had seen too many resurrections. "Let's see. Rumours of a knife in the Senate. The Ides, yes? That narrows it down to—" He calculated, lips moving, "—thirty-seven plausible conspirators and three dozen probable scapegoats."

Decimus watched the list multiply. "I overheard the plan, Hortensius, in the vent. Two senators, one of whom is Marcellus. They think the augurs are compromised, but they're moving anyway. I think they're going to do it."

Hortensius scribbled a circle, drew a line through it. "They always think the augurs are compromised. That's the only way to get things done." He tossed the tablet onto a heap, then poured another cup of wine, this time offering it to Decimus.

He accepted, sipped, and coughed at the taste. It had the chemical bouquet of window cleaner.

"Tell me what you're really afraid of," Hortensius said, voice softer now.

"Nothing, and everything." Decimus traced the rim of the cup. "What if it's true? What if the omens are warnings, not just satire?"

The old man leaned back, balancing on the crate's two rear corners. "You want me to dig, I'll dig." He scanned the shelves, eyes flickering in the flickering half-light, then rose and shuffled to a battered strongbox lashed with copper wire. He fumbled the lock with a set of keys that included, to Decimus's surprise, a fishhook and a chicken bone. The lid creaked open.

Inside were three objects: a scroll sealed in black wax; a mummified hand, also blackened; and a flat stone inscribed with circles and triangles that no bureaucracy on earth could decipher.

Hortensius reverently lifted the scroll and set it between them. "This is the last genuine prophecy to come through the office before they started outsourcing the future to private contractors. I kept a copy. The original, naturally, is missing."

He broke the wax with a thumbnail and unfurled the parchment. Wine stains and mildew had rendered much of it illegible, but enough survived to convey intent.

Decimus read, eyes darting from line to line:

"In the year of the dying eagle, when the river runs backwards,

the Republic shall fall not to arms, but to the hunger of its own children.

A blade will flash within the Senate's womb;

the father's blood will drown the future.

Beware the mouth that says too much,

for it will choke on its own words."

Hortensius traced the last phrase with a trembling finger. "They always wrote these with an eye to interpretation. Still, it has a certain... poetic clarity."

Decimus stared at the ink, which seemed to shimmer in the lamplight. "Why keep it hidden?"

The archivist shrugged. "Because if prophecy mattered, they'd have burned the city a dozen times by now. Also, because I sold the original to a laundress on the black market. She needed it to settle a score with the Temple of Mars." He grinned, displaying the exact number of teeth Decimus had guessed. "And I needed to cover my gambling debts."

Decimus tried to imagine the transaction, failed, and instead asked, "Who was she?"

"Domitia," said Hortensius, as if the name alone explained the city's entropy. "The woman who can wash blood from a toga twice and still leave it stinking of truth." He finished the wine, this time savouring the dregs. "If anyone has the next line in this prophecy, it's her. Or the augurs. But I'd trust the laundress first."

The silence between them thickened, then congealed.

"Why tell me this?" Decimus finally whispered.

The archivist sighed. "Because you're the only scribe I've met who ever bothered to read the footnotes. And because the last three men who asked didn't bother to come back."

He looked up, a ghost of pride flickering on his ruined face. "Take it. I made the copy, I might as well leave a record."

Decimus hesitated, then slipped the prophecy into his sleeve, next to his own growing catalogue of regrets.

"Advice?" he asked, rising.

Hortensius wiped his mouth on his sleeve, then grinned. "Disappear for a month. Failing that, fake your own death. Whichever generates less paperwork."

Decimus started for the door, then looked back. The archivist had already returned to his ledger, scribbling with the precision of a man who knows his work will outlast his name.

The corridor felt longer on the way out. At the threshold, Decimus checked the fragment of prophecy, then the red-threaded scroll. The ink from the old was bleeding into the new. He pressed them together, then let them fall into the lining of his satchel.

A flake of black wax drifted to the floor as he closed the door. He crushed it with his heel, then moved on, determined to walk as quietly as possible.

FOUR

The Office of Divine Permits was located in a wing of the Curia so thoroughly infiltrated by the river that most of the paperwork had the consistency of a funeral shroud. Tribune Scaevola, invited by summons and not by inclination, sat stiffly in a chair borrowed from the adjacent stables, which still retained the imprint and aroma of its last occupant. He regarded the room's other features—leaking amphorae stacked by rank, racks of waterlogged tablets, and a ceiling that wept brackish tears onto the "urgent" in-tray—with the mild horror of a man who has seen an autopsy performed with spoons.

Opposite him, Publius, the appointed Clerk of the Divine Permits (third class), balanced a stack of scrolls against his chest and managed, despite evidence, to project an air of solemnity. His tunic was several shades lighter than decency allowed, his sash knotted with what looked like a child's attempt at maritime signalling, and his hands shook slightly as he bowed, which would have been an affectation if it were not so obviously congenital.

Scaevola, who believed in beginning every conversation as if it were a legal deposition, started: "Your letter indicated discrepancies in the recording of sacrificial privileges. I have brought my own copy of the schedules. I expect you to explain the variance."

Publius blinked, then set the scrolls gently on the desk, where the topmost immediately absorbed a droplet from the overhead leak. "Yes, Tribune. There are... irregularities. The new protocol requires that all divine permits be witnessed, but some of the witnesses have since been disqualified by death. Or, in the case of the Mars temple, by scandal."

Scaevola opened his own folio and thumbed to the appropriate tab. "I see here three permits issued to the Temple of Victory in the last quarter, but no corresponding record of goat expenditure. Explain."

Publius exhaled slowly. "There was a temporary embargo on sacrificial animals. The temple, unable to source live goats, declared bankruptcy on the prior permits. It is all accounted for in the appendix, page twelve."

Scaevola found the page, read the entry, and frowned. "A religious institution cannot declare bankruptcy on a permit. They must submit for extension, or risk retroactive penalty."

The clerk nodded, all too eager. "Of course, Tribune. The penalty is severe, but with the current backlog, it will be years before they are formally censured. By then, the augurs anticipate a new round of reforms, which will make the penalties moot."

The Tribune turned a page. "I see here that a new

temple—the Shrine of Fortunate Errors—received a mass exemption for the Ides. That seems... unusual."

Publius's face underwent a rapid but comprehensive tour of emotional responses, before settling on serene self-absolution. "The exemption was signed by Senator Marcellus's cousin, who is also a registered goat handler. It was witnessed by three secondary augurs and a municipal judge. The documentation is quite robust."

Scaevola scanned the attached signatures. "Two of these witnesses are children. And the municipal judge is under investigation for selling property on consecrated land."

"Nevertheless, the forms are in order." The clerk offered a smile that, in different circumstances, could have been used to coax a confession from a table leg. "The office has learned to anticipate irregularities and incorporate them, pre-emptively, into the record. It ensures a smoother audit process."

Scaevola closed the file. "This is all highly improper. It undermines the chain of accountability and exposes the entire permitting structure to ridicule. I require a full list of all exemptions granted in the past month, cross-referenced by sponsoring official and, if applicable, the colour of wax used in sealing."

Publius bowed again, this time with a hint of personal pride. "Already prepared, Tribune. May I suggest, however, that some of the permits may be... less than authentic?"

"Forgery?" Scaevola's ears caught the word as if they'd been personally insulted.

"Not always deliberate," said the clerk, fidgeting with

a roll of damp parchment. "Occasionally, the sponsor will sign with a surrogate, or a notary will misunderstand the intent. Most forgeries are caught and destroyed, but—" he glanced up, voice lowering "—some reach the Senate."

Scaevola flexed the fingers of his left hand, a tic that had survived two decades of litigation. "If you have evidence of fraud, you will produce it. Now."

Publius hesitated, then, with a conspiratorial flourish, retrieved from his desk's lowest drawer a wax-sealed permit stamped with the emblem of the Office of Official Histories. The seal was uneven, as if impressed by an amateur or in haste, and the parchment, though official in all other respects, smelled faintly of vinegar and burnt feathers.

"This arrived yesterday," said Publius, pushing it across the desk. "I have reason to believe it bypassed the normal channels. The ritual it permits is... unorthodox."

Scaevola broke the seal. The script inside was recognisable at a glance—Decimus Flaccus, who wrote with a half-cursive slant that betrayed his training under the previous regime. The content, however, was disturbing—authorisation for a "mass ritual with potential political consequence," to be staged at the Rostra during the Ides, with special dispensation for the use of "uninspected avian omens."

He scrutinised the closing line. It bore Decimus's name, but the ink was wrong. It had run, as if applied under duress, or with a left hand.

He set the document down, mind already assembling the case.

"I'll need to interview this Flaccus," said Scaevola.

"And any augur who signed off. I also want the list of all staff with access to these files in the last week."

Publius, suddenly less confident, nodded. "I can have it for you by morning. There is, however, one more thing."

Scaevola waited, tapping the wet edge of the permit.

Publius licked his lips. "I saw someone, yesterday. A woman. She was in the archive after hours, asking about old prophecies. I thought it odd, since she had no official badge, but she seemed to know her way around."

"What did she look like?"

The clerk squinted, conjuring the memory. "Tall. Hair like a crow's wing, but eyes blue as the new coins. Carried a laundry basket, but the bottom was false—full of scrolls." He looked up. "She said she was helping with the festival preparations, but her accent was... educated. Not from the city."

Scaevola's mind logged the information. "If you see her again, notify me immediately. And do not, under any circumstances, give her access to restricted documents."

"Yes, Tribune." Publius inclined his head, clearly relieved that responsibility had been successfully redirected.

Scaevola rolled the permit, tucked it into his satchel, and stood. "You will prepare for audit. Any attempt to conceal or destroy records will be met with prosecution."

He strode to the door, then paused. A movement in the corner of his eye—just outside the open archway— caught his attention. A woman, tall and composed, lingered for a fraction of a second before vanishing into the side corridor. Scaevola caught a glimpse of her: hair bound back, posture impeccable, eyes cold as January. The laundress, he assumed. Domitia.

He filed the observation away, then turned back to Publius. "Double the locks on your archive. We have visitors."

Publius nodded, more pallid than before.

Scaevola stepped into the corridor, noting the faintest trace of damp footprints and the residual aroma of strong lye. He followed, careful not to betray his intent. The corridor bent left, then doubled back; by the time he reached the end, the woman was gone. Only a single white thread, snagged on a nail in the lintel, marked her passing.

He collected the thread, wound it around his finger, and smiled.

If Rome was to be saved, it would be by those who understood the patterns—the webwork of forgeries and misplaced faith, the handwriting of men forced to sign their own doom, and the women who passed, unseen, through the gaps.

He returned to his office, the satchel heavy at his side, and began assembling the necessary forms. With luck, and the proper paperwork, even the gods could be made to answer for their errors.

FIVE

The wine-shop, above, was named the Triumph of the Grape—a misnomer, given that nothing grown on a slope could survive the post-diluvian syrup sold here as "vintage." Down the stairs, at the end of a passage barely wide enough for a child or a senator with sufficiently collapsed self-esteem, lay the cellar: a candlelit crypt converted for the urgent practice of unofficial religion.

Decimus Flaccus descended into this sanctum with the reluctance of a man who, invited to dinner, finds himself seated with the guests of honour from his own funeral. The stone steps sweated the previous century's failed harvests, and the walls were padded with mismatched cushions, most of which had been so long in place that their original colour could only be guessed at by forensic dye analysis. The ceiling pressed in, and at its lowest point a fractured amphora collected the drip of what might have been wine, but more likely was the concentrated effluvium of Rome's aquatic infrastructure.

Three people occupied the room. Or, more precisely,

one person and two—possibly three—heretics, for it was hard to judge whether the third was alive, dead, or in some intermediate state induced by proximity to Licinia. She, barefoot and anointed with the ash of whatever ritual had preceded Decimus's arrival, sat cross-legged before an altar of upturned crate and cracked saucer. Her hair hung in streaks, silver and black, and her robes looked as though they'd been acquired, piece by piece, from the city's more discerning rag-pickers.

She greeted him with an upturned palm, not so much beckoning as hailing the next in a queue of the doomed. "Welcome, scribe," said Licinia, voice ringing off the stones with the confidence of a woman certain that the gods took her calls collect. "You are precisely on time, which is to say, late for everything important."

Decimus considered a reply, then discarded it as futile. He skirted the cushions and the spilled wax, careful not to step on any of the cultists or their associated debris. The nearer of the two, a woman with a scholar's beard drawn in lampblack across her jaw, was engaged in the difficult task of separating grape skins from candle stubs in a bowl the size of a helmet. The second, slumped against a pillar and dressed in what might once have been military parade wear, hummed softly to himself while attempting to tie knots in his own sash. The third, a donkey, watched the proceedings with an air of mournful condescension. It was tied to the altar by a length of purple ribbon and chewed on a scroll fragment with what Decimus could only describe as scholarly restraint.

Licinia pointed, as if this required explanation. "It is

for the sacrifice," she said. "But only if the augury is truly dire. Sit."

He obeyed, taking the nearest cushion, which exhaled a gout of dust and wine sediment. He attempted to look dignified, but the seat had other ideas.

Licinia regarded him with the sharpness of someone who saw through layers of history, to the rotten core of each event. "You have come with a question. But the question is not yours. It is the city's."

Decimus braced himself. "I need to know if the threat is real. The omens—there's a rumour, a prophecy, and it matches the date. I have witnesses, but none with credibility. I have forms, but they're all rejected."

Licinia waved a hand. "Credibility is the last refuge of men without vision." She reached behind the altar and produced a cup, which she filled from a jug that had, at some point, been used as a weapon. "Drink."

He hesitated. The last time he'd drunk under compulsion, he'd spent two days in the privy and three more inventing excuses for missed deadlines. He declined with a courteous shake of the head.

She shrugged, downed the cup, and smacked her lips. "Very well. The gods will judge you with a clearer mind than mine."

From the periphery, the bearded woman interjected, "Do you want us to begin the ritual?" Her voice was high and, Decimus suspected, not wholly committed to the present moment.

Licinia glanced at the candle, which was guttering in a pool of wax the colour of old wounds. "Not yet. We must first establish the boundaries of the question." She leaned toward Decimus. "Tell me, in one sentence, what you fear."

He thought for a long moment. "That history will repeat itself," he said. "And I'll be the one footnoted for it."

She nodded, as if this was the answer she'd expected. "The city is made of people like you," she said. "Each terrified of being the one who notices too late. But do you know why history repeats?"

Decimus shook his head.

"Because the scribes are the only ones who remember, and they are always the first to die." She grinned, teeth stained violet. "It's not the best system, but it's the one we have."

She turned to the others. "Now we begin."

The woman with the lampblack beard clapped her hands, then slapped the candle stub into the bowl of grape skins. The man in the military tatters straightened, drew a toy gladius from his belt, and pointed it at the donkey, which ignored him. The donkey, for its part, twitched its ear, then resumed its rumination.

Licinia drew a circle on the flagstones with a slosh of her wine, then motioned for Decimus to extend his hands. He did so, palms up, feeling faintly ridiculous.

"Repeat after me," said Licinia, "May the ears of the city be plugged with wax, but may its eyes be open."

Decimus echoed the phrase, feeling each word settle in his throat like a bad debt.

She sprinkled a pinch of ash onto his left palm. "And may the heart of the city beat only for its own."

Another pinch, onto his right. "And may the blood that flows be accounted for in advance."

The two cultists joined in, mumbling the words and, in the man's case, poking the donkey with the gladius. The donkey finally responded, turning to present its other flank and, with a movement both deliberate and casual, deposited a pile of manure at the edge of the circle.

Licinia beamed. "The sign is auspicious."

She turned to Decimus. "Now, your question. Ask it, but do not use the word 'Caesar.'"

He searched for the right phrasing. "Will the one at the city's heart survive the Ides?"

Licinia considered, then nodded. "Adequate." She closed her eyes and began to chant, a low, rhythmic rumble that reminded Decimus of thunder approaching over flat fields.

The cultists joined in, their voices climbing and colliding, until the sound filled the cellar and seemed to vibrate the stones themselves.

The donkey, perhaps inspired, began to bray in counterpoint.

Decimus closed his own eyes, not out of belief but from the sincere hope that, if he couldn't see the ritual, the ritual couldn't see him.

The chanting ceased as abruptly as it had begun. Licinia opened her eyes, which glowed with the manic clarity of those who have stared too long into fire.

"The future is not a straight road," she said, voice suddenly soft. "It's a blind alley that sometimes doubles back on itself, and sometimes opens into a courtyard full of knives." She reached for his hands, turning them palm up.

"You will survive the Ides," she said, tracing the lines with a finger, "but only as a shadow. The city's heart will stop, and the city will continue. The record will show that you tried, but the footnote will say otherwise." She dropped his hands.

The room fell silent, save for the donkey's steady chewing.

Licinia poured herself another cup. "There. You are now the last man in Rome with a prophecy that matters. Congratulations."

Decimus sat, stunned. He had, in his heart of hearts, expected something less concrete, something easily misfiled. Instead, he'd been handed his own obsolescence.

"Is there anything I can do?" he asked, voice thin as the candlelight.

Licinia shrugged. "You could leave the city. Or you could keep writing. Either way, history will find you."

The bearded woman clapped again, then resumed sorting the grape skins from the wax. The man with the gladius slumped against the pillar, humming softly, his role in the ritual complete.

The donkey, having exhausted the scroll fragment, turned its gaze to Decimus. Its eyes, deep and unblinking, seemed to hold the whole of the city's future and its past.

He stood, not without effort, and prepared to leave. Licinia paused in her preparations, considered him with a strange, almost maternal affection, and said, "If you really want answers, you'll come to the Festival of Intoxicated Mars. There's a proper ritual, with masks and figs and so much screaming. Bring your own wine."

He nodded, already edging towards the door. As he reached the threshold, Licinia's voice followed: "I saw you in another dream. You were washing blood from linen, and a woman was watching. There was a curtain, and you were on the wrong side."

Decimus mumbled something like thanks, stumbled up the stairs, and out into the unsteady night. The air was, if anything, thicker outside the shrine, but at least it did not contain so much omen.

He ascended, the weight of the prophecy pressing him down even as he climbed. At the threshold of the wine shop, he paused, listening to the muffled bray echo up from below.

It sounded, for the first time, exactly like his own voice.

The Senate Archives were at their finest in the hours after sunset, when the day's breed of opportunists and loiterers had retreated to the wine stalls or their mistresses, and only the ghosts and their janitors remained. Lucilla Minor, whose patience for ghosts far outstripped her patience for the living, preferred to work then. The echo in the empty corridors—part scurrying rodent, part memory—reminded her that, at least among the stacks, the past was safely dead and could not touch her.

She sat at the main desk in the High Record Vault, the night's silence broken only by the scritch of her pen and the slow combustion of a tallow candle that had already been pressed to overtime. The ledgers before her were a triple column of shame, each line a story of money spent, lost, or recalculated out of existence. She ran a finger down the page, counting not in sestertii but in potential scaffolds and funerary monuments.

From the deepest shadows, a slouch announced the arrival of Cassius, her assigned scribe and, in any meaningful sense, the city's only investment in her continued existence. He was a boy whose ambition had been thoroughly corroded by exposure to Senate bureaucracy, and whose only remaining virtues were a capacity for trivial memorisation and the stamina to survive on two hours' sleep a week.

"Madam," Cassius yawned, "the new intake is processed. Unless the office rats have developed opposable thumbs, in which case we're all doomed."

Lucilla grunted, a noise she'd perfected in place of greetings. She didn't look up from the ledger. "Anything from the Triumvirate?"

"A packet of decrees, two festival invitations, and a tray of honeyed biscuits from 'the Office of Official Histories—urgent and confidential.'" He dropped the biscuits on her desk, where they shattered into their constituent sugars. "Should I check them for poison?"

She allowed herself the faintest twitch of a smile. "No, they don't fear me enough for poison. Not yet. If anything, it will be a bribe disguised as a compliment— and probably stale."

Cassius perched on a stool, arranging himself into a shape optimised for minimum exertion. "Is it true what they say about the new Calendar Project? That it's costing more than the annual flood mitigation?"

Lucilla didn't answer, not because the question was insipid—though it was—but because she'd just traced a line in the ledger that disagreed with reality. The entry read: "Public Works, Via Appia South—funds redirected, see AUCTUM – Solis Planum (Phase I)." She frowned, then leafed back a dozen pages. Each time a civic project vanished from the records, the destination was the same: AUCTUM – Solis Planum.

She said, "Cassius. When you processed the decrees, did you see anything about 'Solis Planum'?"

Cassius cocked his head. "The name's in the current roster. Temple construction, expedited schedule. Caesar's personal seal on the order." He blinked, then shrugged. "Rumour is, it's a new forum or a calendar temple. Nobody cares which, so long as they get paid."

Lucilla closed the ledger, the pages smacking together like a trap. "It's not in the census. It's not in the infrastructure list. And yet every unallocated denarius in the city is draining into it." She pointed her pen at Cassius, as though marking him for audit. "Find me the original application. I want to know who signed off."

He groaned, then padded into the labyrinth of document shelves. Lucilla waited, scanning the candlelit gloom. The walls rose up in tiers of pigeonhole cubbies, each jammed with scrolls or wax tablets labelled in a variety of hands and tempers. Some tags were aspirational ("Infrastructure: Pending"), others resigned ("Prophecies (Class D)"), and some simply pleaded for an end ("Senate Complaints – Burned 2x").

She absently crumbled a honeyed biscuit and scattered it on the flagstones, where a pair of archive lizards scuttled out to squabble over the spoils.

Cassius returned, holding a sheaf of requisition slips bound with twine. He dropped them on the desk. "Found it. And several duplicates. Some are counter-signed by Marcus the Minor, some by a woman called 'Domitia, Agent-at-Large.' Not standard procedure."

Lucilla rifled through the slips, eyebrows arching fractionally at each impropriety. "Domitia," she said. "Isn't that the laundress who threatened the Temple of Mars?"

Cassius shrugged. "It's possible. She has very neat handwriting for a criminal."

Lucilla worked through the pages, then pointed to a line near the bottom. "Look at the date. All construction halts on the Ides. After that, nothing."

He peered at it, then back at her. "So?"

"So," Lucilla said, voice sharpening, "someone is funnelling every possible resource into a project that doesn't exist on the records, then ending it abruptly the day Rome expects a public spectacle." She let the silence hang. "Either the world's largest birthday cake is about to debut, or someone is planning something that requires a blank spot in the calendar."

Cassius considered, then nodded. "Could be both, knowing this city."

She rolled up the requisitions, tucked them under her arm, and extinguished the candle with a practiced pinch. "I want the entire archive of Ides-related omens on my desk before dawn," she said. "Also, cross-check all outgoing correspondence for mentions of 'calendar realignment' or 'augur interference.'"

He groaned, but didn't argue.

Lucilla slipped into the corridor, the stone cold against her sandals. She kept the requisition bundle tight, as if the Fates themselves had tied the cords. The echo of her steps was joined by the soft, uncertain tread of the city's other insomniacs. She passed the locked office of the Office of Official Histories, paused for a moment at its door, then moved on, up the stair and out into the colonnade.

Above, the moon hung low and dull. The city was asleep, or pretending to be. Lucilla regarded the empty Forum, the scattered torches, and the distant sound of a donkey braying from somewhere near the wine district.

She closed her eyes and committed the pattern to memory. In the morning, she would have answers. And if not, she would have the documentation to make the next generation regret it.

Behind her, Cassius appeared, arms full of prophecy scrolls, eyes still half-closed. He offered her one at random. "First batch," he said. "This one's in code. I think it's Greek."

She took it, unrolled it, and read the first line. "When the sun is stabbed, its shadow will multiply," she translated. "Typical."

They stood in silence, the dawn yet an hour off, but the future already groaning to life behind the stacks.

Lucilla glanced at the sky, then at Cassius, and said, "Let's get to work."

SIX

The street outside Domitia's laundry presented itself as a contest between aromas: the competing stench of boiled lye and sacrificial by-products, each intensified by the afternoon sun, and a top-note of ancient goat from the tanner's two doors down. Decimus Flaccus, toga-less and with the self-assurance of a man forced to brave the world in a borrowed bedsheet, squeezed himself through the courtyard's low archway and into the steamy, clamorous world within.

The first impression was of linen, not merely as object but as atmosphere. Damp sheets hung overhead in taut, shifting arrays, their pallor lending the space the light quality of a fever dream. Underfoot, the paving was slick with run-off, and every surface not covered by textile was either scalding to the touch or rendered soapy and treacherous by overenthusiastic rinsing. Among this, the washerwomen moved with a choreographed violence, their arms and voices rising and falling in synchrony as they battered laundry against stone, grunted in time with the blows, and occasionally hurled insults at each other that echoed the city's more sophisticated epithets in abridged form.

At the centre of the operation, Domitia presided from behind a makeshift table piled with folded garments, her gaze switching between a ledger and the yard's slow-motion skirmish. She wore a practical version of the city's standard attire—stained at the edges, cinched at the waist with a sash that looked capable of garrotting a small mammal—and her hair, despite the humidity, remained precisely controlled. Only the set of her mouth betrayed any amusement at the proceedings.

"Flaccus," she called, before he'd properly crossed the threshold. "Early today. Did your last meeting go short, or are you hiding from the archives again?"

Decimus offered a smile, which failed to impress. "Neither. I was hoping to collect my toga before the evening chill. If it's—"

Domitia's fingers snapped. "Vibia!" she called, without looking round. "Check the top line—white with red trim, no sweat stains, account paid." A girl emerged from the steam, handed over a crisp roll of cloth, and retreated without making eye contact.

Domitia proffered the toga as though extending a challenge. "You don't usually come yourself," she said. "Did you get lost?"

He took the toga and unrolled it, feigning a meticulous inspection. "I wanted to see the progress," he said. "And to be sure you hadn't given up on the more difficult stains." He caught the faint odour—slightly resinous, with an undertone of something burnt.

Domitia's eyes narrowed in good-natured accusation. "You've been attending sacrifices again. I told you: the blood goes in, the blood comes out, and the toga's never the same." She dusted her hands. "But that's not why you're here."

He coughed, then smoothed the cloth against his arm. "Is it not customary to collect one's own garments? I've been warned about the risks of intermediaries." He regretted the remark instantly, but Domitia seemed to relish it.

"Risks, yes. Especially with the current mood in the city." She jerked her head at the courtyard, where one of the washerwomen was now haranguing a neighbour for misidentifying a type of wine stain. "It only takes a single mistake to end up ruined. Professionally, or otherwise." She placed her palms flat on the table, leaning forward just enough to suggest that he was now the focus of her entire afternoon. "You know, we get all sorts through here. Priests, scribes, senators' nephews—sometimes even the real thing. And the gossip is better than the wine."

Decimus glanced at the exit, then at the stack of clean garments between them. "I'm not much for gossip," he said, rearranging the toga with more enthusiasm than skill. "The truth is usually less exciting, and harder to wash out."

Domitia gave a low, amused hum. "I disagree. For example: a scribe from the Office of Official Histories, visiting both the ex-augur and the disgraced archivist in a single day? Even I can smell a story there." She punctuated this with a raised eyebrow and the faintest suggestion of a smile.

Decimus's left hand began a traitorous dance along the toga's hem, while his right dabbed at a bead of sweat at his brow. "I have no idea what you mean," he said, but the words ran together, and he had the unpleasant feeling that even the cauldrons were judging his performance.

Domitia, not one to prolong suffering without purpose, waved a hand. "Relax, Flaccus. If I wanted to ruin you, I'd have done it before your hair started thinning. You're not the first to traffic in secrets, and you won't be the last." She lowered her voice. "But you should know: the women here see everything. And what they don't see, they invent. Even now, they're watching us and wondering whether you've come to confess, or to recruit."

He managed a laugh, thin and uneven. "If the city ever comes to its senses, it will let the washerwomen run it."

"Give it a month," said Domitia. "The way the Senate is going, they'll be lucky if they're still laundering their own reputations." She swept her ledger closed, then fixed him with a more serious gaze. "Is there a reason you're visiting today, of all days? Did you need something more than your toga?"

He hesitated, then shook his head. "No. I only—" He searched for the end of the sentence and, not finding it, let the silence build.

Domitia tilted her head. "You've been seen with Licinia." It wasn't a question.

"She's the only augur who makes sense," said Decimus, then realised too late that this was damning in itself.

Domitia's voice softened, but only fractionally. "Be

careful with that one. She makes sense because she's done pretending to care about anyone else's."

He nodded, then dropped his eyes to the table, tracing the grain with his thumb. "Thank you for the warning."

Domitia tapped the ledger with a knuckle. "If you need something cleaned—really cleaned—you come here. Otherwise, try not to get anything on the white bits." She returned to her accounts, the conversation closed as abruptly as it had begun.

Decimus lingered a moment, then gathered his toga and made for the archway. As he passed between the steaming vats, one of the washerwomen, a slip of a girl with forearms like bundled rope, murmured, "That's him, then?" Her companion, older and carrying a bowl of caustic paste, glanced after him with open curiosity.

Domitia, not looking up from her sums, said, "Let him run a bit longer." She smiled to herself, or to the ledger, or to whatever network of eyes and ears already raced ahead of Decimus through the city.

He stepped out into the alley, the evening's first breeze finding him damp at the collar. He draped the toga over his arm, inhaling its impossible whiteness, and hurried on—knowing that, for the rest of the night, he would not be able to tell whether he was running from something or towards it.

By the hour when the city's serious business devolved into gossip and posturing, the south steps of the Forum became a holding pen for Rome's lesser dignitaries, minor functionaries, and the entire genus of citizen whose importance was measurable only in decibels. Decimus, toga draped over one arm and a thrum in his chest that suggested nothing good awaited him at home, found himself swept along in this confluence of official idleness.

At the top of the steps, a knot of message runners and interns jostled for position, their voices volleying news of decrees, petitions, and scandal with the reckless abandon of men paid by the word. The sunlight, sharpening as it slid down the stone, illuminated motes of dust and the fluttering of wax-sealed scrolls. A donkey, tethered loosely to a signpost advertising the merits of a certain municipal candidate, tugged persistently at its lead, aiming itself with the stoic patience of the doomed toward the nearest unattended basket of apricots.

Tribune Scaevola, in full civic plumage, stood at the centre of this moving tableau. He held himself with such absolute verticality that lesser men developed spinal pain merely watching. His eyes, pale as watered wine, fixed on the miscreants before him with the intensity of a celestial event.

"Rome does not pause for personal inconvenience," he intoned, as two scribes in ill-matched tunics attempted to explain why a marble plinth, delivered for tomorrow's Ides festivities, had been installed upside-down. "Nor," continued Scaevola, "does it tolerate idleness dressed as confusion. There is a process. Observe it."

The more talkative scribe, red in the face and

sweating despite the mildness, pointed with both hands at the offending monument. "With respect, Tribune, the guidelines for plinth orientation are inconsistent between the east and west quadrants. And the diagrams—"

Scaevola raised a hand for silence, and silence obeyed. "The diagrams," he said, "were approved by the Consul's Office. If you wish to challenge the Consul's interpretation of verticality, I suggest you pursue another line of work. Or," he allowed a rare smile to crack his face, "a horizontal one."

The crowd exhaled a collective snicker; the donkey brayed, as if on cue.

From the bottom of the steps, Decimus watched the proceedings with the detachment of a man reviewing his own autopsy. He noted that, for all the apparent disorder, there was a rhythm to the chaos—a cycle of blunder, correction, and threatened demotion that kept the empire more or less on schedule. It was, he thought, a comfort of sorts, to know that disaster could be postponed indefinitely by the careful misfiling of forms.

His reverie was interrupted by a commotion to his right. A runner, pale and panting, crashed through the perimeter with a bundle of loose scrolls, scattering insults and apologies in equal measure. At his heels stumbled a man in chains, whose toga was shredded to the point of impropriety and whose face bore the resigned clarity of a man for whom all hope had already been itemised and stamped.

Scaevola turned his attention to the condemned, who, on seeing the Tribune, attempted to stand at something approximating attention. The runner dropped the scrolls at the Tribune's feet and gasped: "Provisional Guilty, pending escalation! Sir—he says the execution notice was misfiled!"

The chained man nodded, then spat on the steps. "I demand the right to appeal. You're all using the wrong forms. Check the date—check the date, you paper-humping bastard!"

The crowd tensed, awaiting Scaevola's response. The Tribune bent, retrieved the topmost scroll, and, without looking up, said, "The date is correct. So is the sentence." He snapped the scroll closed. "If you persist, I'll have you downgraded to Pre-emptive Loss, with no hope of post-humous rectification. Is that what you want?"

The man in chains trembled, and for a moment, Decimus thought he might collapse. But he rallied, squaring his shoulders with surprising dignity. "You never even looked at the form," he said.

Scaevola did not deign to answer. Instead, he signalled the nearest lictor, who seized the man's elbow and began the business of shepherding him toward the holding cell, conveniently situated next to the sausage vendor. The man glanced back, his eyes catching Decimus's for a fraction of a second—a moment that contained, for Decimus, all the possibility of his own future.

As the spectacle dispersed, Decimus found himself shunted closer to Scaevola by the indifferent crowd. He could hear, now, the Tribune's side-mutter to his attendant: "—this city would run smooth as olive oil if it weren't for the people required to operate it." The attendant nodded with practiced agreement, scribbling notes on a wax tablet with such fervour that flakes of wax pattered down like black snow.

A bell tolled from the direction of the temple, and the crowd thinned as swiftly as it had formed. Vendors returned to their bickering, the donkey recommenced its siege of the apricots, and the afternoon light faded to a more forgiving hue.

Decimus, seeing his path to escape, made to leave. But a sensation of being observed—distinct from the ambient surveillance of city life—stopped him. He glanced up the steps and caught, among the departing officials, a figure in a hooded mantle. The man, or possibly woman, stood perfectly still, half-shrouded by the portico's shadow. The face, indistinct, seemed to be aimed not at the Forum but directly at Decimus.

He looked away, then back. The figure had vanished.

His heart, already inclined to panic, made a credible effort at flight. He adjusted his toga, wrapped it round himself for the appearance of composure, and strode up the steps, past the Tribune and his assistant. As he did, he caught a snatch of their conversation:

"—watch that one," said Scaevola, low enough to pass for rumour. "He's not nearly as harmless as he appears."

The assistant looked up, blinked, then scribbled something more on the tablet.

Decimus did not stop to consider whether the words were meant for him. He fixed his eyes on the end of the colonnade, where the shadow thickened into night, and walked faster. His pace carried him into the city's arteries, through a backwash of departing petitioners, hawkers packing their trays, and a gang of children playing dice with a severed chicken foot.

Halfway to the next intersection, his progress was checked by the sudden intrusion of a goat, which materialised from an alley and struck him in the thigh with the force of well-meaning bureaucracy. Decimus stumbled, the toga twisting round his knees, and crashed into a tray of sausages, which clattered to the ground with a sound like distant applause.

He apologised to the vendor, who glared, then at the goat, which merely continued eating the scroll it had found. Behind him, the city's light dimmed, and the sense of surveillance faded, or perhaps merely changed hands.

He gathered himself, straightened the toga, and hurried on—certain, for the second time that day, that he was being run to ground by powers neither ancient nor especially interested in his continued existence.

From somewhere far off, the donkey brayed again, a sound that struck Decimus as uncannily like laughter.

SEVEN

Sub-Archive 3B had never been built; it had simply occurred, the product of centuries of shifting ledgers, damp, and the kind of architectural compromise only achieved by a bureaucracy too parsimonious to admit that marble and silt were fundamentally incompatible. The descent required no less than four turns, each more abrupt than the last, with torchlight growing sicklier until it was uncertain whether the walls sweated more from the climate or the fear of what crept within them. At the base, a bronze plaque labelled "3B – Incident Repositories" was affixed at chest height, as if daring the user to claim they hadn't seen it.

Decimus Flaccus arrived at the threshold feeling not unlike a centurion dispatched to negotiate with a particularly unwashed tribe. He paused, inhaled the air—a blend of mildew, vinegar ink, and the sweet rot of neglected leather—and ducked inside.

The anteroom consisted of two desks, a locked grate, and a series of shelves sagging under the weight of scrolls so old they appeared to be reverting to papyrus. The torches here burned unevenly, lending each corner its own distinct region of shadow. A pair of slippers—navy blue, with little rabbit heads sewn onto the toes—protruded from behind the larger desk. Their owner, a man of uncertain years and even less certain hygiene, had managed to nap while upright, head cradled in a nest of forms.

Decimus rapped his knuckles on the desk. The archivist awoke with the expression of one who had never seen the sun but knew it existed chiefly as a threat to one's paperwork. He focused with effort, then blinked several times as if scrolling through an internal catalogue.

"Name and purpose?" he croaked, voice engineered for maximum dryness.

"Flaccus, Decimus. Retrieval on behalf of the Senate's Office of Official Histories. Speech scroll, reference point 'Oratio On Reallocation of City Fountains', Consular Year 811."

The archivist—Publius, according to his ink-smudged lapel—gave a short, mirthless laugh. "That's a cold case. Senator in question died two years ago, probably of the speech." He levered himself up, adjusted the sash round his waist, and peered at Decimus with a myopic squint. "You will not find what you're seeking in the main stacks. Try the annex."

"I was told," said Decimus, "that all annexes below the first are sealed for audit."

"They are," said Publius, "unless you bring your own fire hazard." He eyed the lamp Decimus carried, then jerked his head toward the east corridor. "Annex three.

The speech will be in the section marked 'Misattribu-tions'. If you touch anything else, log it and return in the same condition you found it."

Decimus inclined his head. "Is there a sign-in?"

Publius produced a battered ledger and plonked it onto the counter. Decimus signed, receiving in return a glance of such deep scepticism that it could have been weaponised.

The passage to Annex 3 was so low even Decimus, not a tall man, had to stoop. The walls oozed; the floor alternated between ancient tile and exposed, angry dirt. He passed a puddle of indeterminate origin, skirted a heap of what appeared to be petrified newsletters, and arrived at a gate fastened by nothing more complicated than a slipknot and a bureaucrat's sense of security.

The annex itself resembled an ossuary designed by mad librarians. Scrolls lined every wall, bundled by twine, stuffed into amphorae, or crammed in piles that formed their own unsteady topography. There was a desk, the kind that might once have been used to conduct rituals or exorcisms, and beside it, a wooden crate labelled, in large, hopeful print: "RETURN TO PUBLIUS."

He set the lamp down, then began the search. At first, he stuck to the assignment—"Oratio On Reallocation of City Fountains"—but his hands, infected by years of rummaging through the detritus of Roman government, soon wandered to more interesting materials. There was a case file on "Alleged Owl Malfeasance", which, on closer inspection, contained mostly doodles of owls. A sheaf labelled "Confiscated Wedding Toasts – Sloppy" held exactly what it promised, with marginal notes like "defamatory" and "unoriginal" written in red ink.

As he worked, he became increasingly aware of a persistent itch beneath his collar, which was either the product of archival dust or the knowledge that somewhere above, Publius probably maintained a log of every minute spent in the annex. He took comfort in the fact that the man seemed too lazy to act on it.

Roughly halfway through a box labelled "Classified: Misfiled", Decimus's thumb caught on a scroll whose tag looked freshly glued. He tugged it free. The handwriting on the label was his own. Not similar—identical, down to the slightly flamboyant cross of the "f" and the habit of abbreviating the year in the lower corner. The date corresponded to a week when, officially, Decimus had been out with a mild case of ritual poisoning.

The scroll itself was double-wrapped and sealed in a brittle envelope that declared, in bold script: "MORAL MEMORY DO NOT READ." On the back, someone had scrawled "Class C – Prophetia. Do not circulate." Decimus's fingers tingled.

He unwrapped it, the sound dangerously loud in the hush. The first few lines were, as he suspected, written in his own hand, but the content was unfamiliar.

He read:

"In the year of the divided eagle, when even the augurs fear their own birds,

History will be edited not by the victor, but by the one who survives the audit.

The knife will return to the hand that wrote it, and the city will bleed footnotes.

*Beware the scribe who tells the truth before it happens:
He will be made history's first casualty."*

He sat back, pulse ticking in his neck. The implication was obvious, and unwelcome. He checked the bottom margin, which bore the familiar stamp of the Office of Official Histories, but the attestation line was left blank.

He reached for his satchel, rummaged, and found the "Ides" warning scroll—still tucked, inconspicuously, in the lining. He compared the two, line by line. They matched, word for word, except the one he held now added a final sentence:

"It is the fate of Rome to mistake warnings for instructions."

He was pondering this when a soft noise, the sort that accompanied the slow-motion collapse of minor government, announced the arrival of Hortensius.

The old archivist materialised from the shadows, as if built from them. His robe was damp at the hems, and a band of nervous perspiration had slicked his forehead to near transparency. He looked at the scroll in Decimus's hand, then at Decimus, then back to the scroll, and managed a grimace that could have been mistaken for a smile.

"Put that down," Hortensius whispered. "It was never meant to return."

Decimus, at a loss, did not comply. "Is this the missing prophecy?" he asked, low as he dared.

Hortensius advanced, one step, then another. "It's a copy. Of a copy. The original was burned. But nobody told the system to stop duplicating it."

He reached for the scroll, hands trembling. Decimus jerked it back. "Is it yours?" he asked.

The old man shook his head, beads of sweat spraying like the after-effect of a sneeze. "No one's. It belongs to the city now. And if it's found—if the right person sees it —things fall apart faster than Caesar's virtue."

Decimus weighed his options. "Why is it here? Why my hand, my label?"

Hortensius hissed, "That's the system. It's always the system. You're the best at what you do, Flaccus, but you're not the only one who can be made to sign."

"Who else has seen it?"

Hortensius's glance ricocheted round the annex. "No one who would admit it. But I've heard the rumours. They're using this—this artifact—to justify a cleansing. Of inconvenient facts. Of people. They're going to reset the record, and we'll be the footnotes."

A cough echoed down the corridor, followed by the approach of footsteps: slow, deliberate, dragging.

"Publius," whispered Decimus.

Hortensius's eyes bulged. "If he sees you with that, we're both—"

The steps paused at the threshold. Publius's voice, nasal and unimpressed, carried across the room: "Gentlemen, archive hours are posted for a reason."

Decimus, in a flurry, tucked the scroll inside the catering invoice he'd brought for annotation. Hortensius straightened, wiped his brow on his sleeve, and assumed the pose of a man whose only secret was a mild ulcer.

Publius entered, holding a tray of cold barley cakes. "Break's over," he announced. "You'll need to clear the annex—some junior auditors are coming down to check the fire suppression." He sneezed, twice, then turned to Decimus. "Did you find your speech?"

"I did," said Decimus, grabbing the first scroll in reach, which happened to be a treatise on "Effective Pavement Drainage."

"Fine, fine. Just sign it out and leave everything else untouched. Some of us take the integrity of the record seriously." Publius plodded off, tray balanced on his paunch.

Decimus waited until the footsteps faded, then drew close. "What do I do with it," he whispered.

"Meet me at Taverna Minerva, we'll talk more."

Decimus nodded, then watched as the old man shuffled off, merging once again with the darkness.

He stayed a moment longer, letting the silence fill him. The archive had returned to its previous condition: damp, half-lit, and indifferent to the fates of the men who wandered through it.

He took the prophecy scroll, now carefully wrapped in the invoice, and secured it in his satchel. He logged the treatise as instructed, then headed for the exit, careful to avoid puddles, dust traps, and anything else liable to remember him.

As he signed out, Publius looked up from his desk, eyes oddly lucid. "You know," he said, "they say every scribe in this city is just an unpaid augur. Do you believe that?"

"Not yet," said Decimus.

Publius smiled, the kind of smile that suggested nothing good for anyone. "You will."

Decimus left, the prophecy burning in his satchel, the echoes of the annex following him up each step.

Outside, the evening air felt fresher, if only by comparison. Decimus squared his shoulders, already dreading the next request, the next speech, the next lie he would be asked to bury.

He set off, toward the city and its infinite appetite for history, unaware that behind him, in the damp heart of the archive, a new copy of the scroll was already being made.

The Taverna Minerva was the sort of establishment where ambitions went to ferment. Its entrance, once grandly flanked by statuettes of the goddess herself, was now half-obscured by the awning of a sardine vendor, and the interior design suggested that, at some stage, the owner had received a discount on marble-effect plaster and failed fresco restoration. Decimus Flaccus chose it less for the quality of its fare than for its reputation as the one tavern in the city where a man might be left to drown his misfortunes in private, provided he paid cash and did not attempt to convert the wait staff.

He arrived early, selecting the booth most distant from both the kitchen and the privy. The table was sticky and bore a mosaic of previous indignities—wine stains, charred bread, the outline of what might have been a sacrificial chicken but was more likely a careless hand. He settled in, spread the prophecy scroll and the catering invoice on the bench beside him, and ordered the house special: lentil stew and a cup of whatever passed for the goddess's nectar. The waiter—Titus, according to the battered badge on his sash—nodded with the enthusiasm of a man counting the minutes to closing time.

Hortensius appeared with none of his usual theatre. He entered hunched, eyes darting to every darkened corner, as if expecting a deputation from the Ministry of Moral Memory to leap from the pot plants. He slid into the booth, flinching at the contact with the seat, and offered Decimus a nod that was all apology and no greeting.

"You're late," said Decimus.

"I'm always late," replied Hortensius, gaze fixed on the grain of the table. "It's the only way to ensure one's absence is noticed."

Decimus produced the scroll, leaving it partly shrouded in the invoice. Hortensius recoiled, then leaned in, lowering his voice until it was barely audible over the clatter from the kitchen.

"You don't understand," he whispered. "If anyone sees you with that, we're—"

"I have no intention of waving it around," said Decimus. "But I want the truth. Why is my hand on this? Why is it in the archive? And why does every augur, priest, and functionary in the city seem to know it exists, but not what it means?"

Hortensius closed his eyes, breathed once, and exhaled defeat. "It was a plant," he said. "A fake. A calculated fiction, meant to discredit the soothsayers who— how do I put this—got too creative with their forecasts.

There was an... operation. They called it Project Cassandra, because even the censors have a sense of humour." He winced. "It was meant to be a joke."

"A joke?" said Decimus, louder than intended. From the next booth, an elderly couple paused their argument to listen.

Hortensius winced again, and spoke more quietly. "A diversion. Who listens to basement augurs? But if you make enough noise, and float the right rumour, suddenly the official prophecies start to look... less convenient. The hope was, the Ministry would cite the scroll, discredit the rival augurs, and bury the lot in a standard audit."

"And instead?" asked Decimus.

"Instead," said Hortensius, "someone took it literally. There's a coterie of hotheads who think it's not just prophecy, but sanction. They think it's an instruction, not a warning." He sipped at the water Titus had deposited, then grimaced and set the glass down. "If that scroll gets cited in the wrong context, it becomes gospel. And gospel has consequences."

The stew arrived. It was less a meal than a dare: congealed, tepid, and decorated with a single withered bay leaf. Decimus ignored it.

"Why my hand?" he asked. "Why not some hack from the scriptoria?"

Hortensius's cheeks tinged pink. "Because you have a reputation. You're precise. They said, 'Let Flaccus do it—he'll make it plausible.' I tried to warn them, but you know how the system works."

Decimus stared, appetite gone. "What happens now?"

Hortensius shook his head, then eyed the booth's partition with fresh suspicion. "Depends who finds it first. If the Senate's censors get it, they'll burn it and claim it was never there. If the wrong augur gets it, they'll read it at a public ceremony and then—" he made a cutting gesture "—Rome will bleed footnotes for a generation."

Titus returned, this time with a carafe and two chipped cups. "You gentlemen doing all right?" he asked, drawing out the last word and glancing pointedly at the scroll.

"We're fine," said Decimus.

Titus set the carafe down, then lingered, fingers drumming the table. "You know, I heard something today in the Forum. Someone reciting a verse about knives and scribes, and the city's fate. Sounded like a play, but the crowd ate it up." He shrugged, face bright with the hope of being included.

Decimus paled. "What exactly did you hear?"

Titus grinned. "Went something like, 'The knife will return to the hand that wrote it, and the city will bleed footnotes.' Gave me a chill, to be honest." He reached for the carafe, poured himself a thimbleful, and toasted them. "Not every day you hear a prophecy before the Ides."

He departed, leaving the two men in a silence that was anything but private. From several tables, faces now openly watched them. The acoustics, as always, were terrible for secrets.

Hortensius massaged his temples. "It's started," he said. "Once it's on the street, it can't be called back. By tomorrow, half the city will be parroting it, and the other half will be writing it into law."

Decimus wanted to argue, but knew better. He reached for the scroll, then thought better of it. "If I destroy it?"

Hortensius snorted. "You can't destroy an idea, Flaccus. Especially not one Rome finds amusing. We're the only city on earth that sees its destiny as a punchline."

He looked up, suddenly tired beyond years. "If it's any comfort, I don't think history will blame you. You're too careful, too... footnoted."

Decimus met his eyes, saw in them the bleak camaraderie of men who knew their futures would be appended in red ink, after the fact.

They sipped from the carafe, neither tasting the wine, both straining to hear the latest rumour as it echoed through the city, gaining weight and momentum.

From the kitchen, a crash. From the street, a burst of laughter, then the chanting of a children's rhyme, which, though mangled, still carried the new gospel:

The knife returns to the hand that wrote it—

and Rome will bleed footnotes.

Decimus closed his eyes. In the darkness, the words repeated, irrepressible and, by now, utterly unstoppable.

Outside, the city rumbled and prepared itself for tomorrow, ready to repeat history in whatever new and dreadful pattern it could invent.

EIGHT

Senator Lucilla Minor had prepared her statement for the Subcommittee on Civic Infrastructure as if her future depended on it, which, in several measurable senses, it did. The chamber into which she now entered was a rotunda of such calculated mediocrity that one could have reconstructed the entire history of municipal Rome from its visible failures: the crevices in the imported marble, the flaking gilt on every horizontal surface, the legion of misaligned busts commemorating men who had never attended a meeting sober. Above the dais, a frieze depicted the Founding of the Forum by means of three nude demigods and a suspiciously erect aqueduct, the latter added in the most recent restoration at the personal insistence of Senator Veturius.

She found her seat, straightened the hem of her conservative, unsmeared tunic, and surveyed the opposition. There were twelve senators present, of whom eight were awake. The Chairman, an ambulant pudding named Piso, had forsworn sleeves in favour of a decorative stole that suggested both lineage and a dietary reliance on root vegetables. His colleagues dozed in an order that mirrored the time of day—Veteran senators slumped after lunch, the Juniors drifting just before dusk, and the Elder Emeriti preserving energy for the main event, which was lunch, but with an audience.

Lucilla waited for silence, and then, with the rhetorical force of a woman who had spent too many evenings diagramming the city's failures on her bedroom ceiling, began.

"My proposal," she said, "is a two-pronged approach to the present water crisis. First, immediate redirection of funds from the suspended statuary refurbishment to the repair of the Aqua Marcia and its two major branches—"

"Point of order," croaked Senator Veturius, who had previously been observed napping through his own daughter's wedding. "Is the statuary refurbishment actually suspended? I was led to believe the project was merely... recalibrated."

Lucilla allowed the interruption, only because experience had taught her that resisting would double its length. "The project is technically active, but the last three statuary shipments arrived pre-damaged, and the city's masons are on indefinite strike."

"Then what," said Veturius, lips twitching with the effort of subterfuge, "do you propose the sculptors do in the meantime? Idle hands—" Here he paused, perhaps to remember the saying, or perhaps in the hope that someone else would finish it for him. "—are a resource squandered. It's not the Roman way."

Chairman Piso, eyes darting between Lucilla and

Veturius with all the decisiveness of a leaf in a puddle, motioned for the record-keeper to note the concern.

Lucilla pressed on. "If we do not address the main breach in the Marcia, I estimate, with respect, that the city's central fountains will dry within a week. Citizens rely on these for drinking, for sanitation, for the appearance—however notional—of civic stability."

She had meant to deliver this last line as a calculated barb, but it fell flat amid the audible snoring from Subcommittee Scribe #2. Someone's pigeon, long since promoted from mascot to member, shuffled on the windowsill and excreted a contribution to the debate.

Veturius, emboldened by the chairman's lack of spine, sat forward. "Senator Minor, would you care to comment on the... ahem, rumour of excessive pigeon population contributing to the fouling of the city's aqueducts? It has reached my office that the birds are, shall we say, supplementing the city's water with their own... effluents."

Lucilla inhaled, then let the exhale carry her patience with it. "With respect, the pigeons have always supplemented the aqueduct. The present difference is that they outnumber the city's administrators."

Veturius grinned, pleased with himself for having scored a point that he neither understood nor intended. "Very well, then. Let the record show that the bird issue is, for now, unsolvable."

The Quills, three identical junior aides in matching tunics and haircuts, scribbled this down in perfect synchrony. They had been hired for their penmanship and, in the process, had lost the capacity for independent thought.

Lucilla steered the debate back to its stated purpose. "The second prong is legislative: a temporary stay on all new festivals or commemorations requiring water displays until the Marcia is repaired. The calendar is already at capacity with invented holidays; I see no reason to dilute our efforts further."

At this, the room awoke, as if the words "holidays" and "dilute" had rung an internal bell.

Chairman Piso blinked, then said, "Is it legal to postpone a festival once it has been scheduled?"

"Only," said Lucilla, "if a majority of the Subcommittee ratifies the stay, and the matter is countersigned by the relevant augur or, failing that, the Office of the Divine Calendar."

She had them. For a moment.

But Veturius, whose approach to logic was best measured in cubits, swooped in. "On the subject of festivals, I must inform the Subcommittee that Caesar's Office has issued a countermand. The funds for the Marcia repair have already been... repurposed, toward a new civic project of the highest priority."

Lucilla did not blink. "Documentation, please."

Veturius produced a scroll, unbroken seal and all. The Quills shuffled closer, bearing it like an offering to the gods of intransigence. "Read it aloud," he commanded.

Quill #1 broke the seal and, in a voice as nasal as a caged goose, recited: "Pursuant to the Decree of Public

Alignment, all expenditures earmarked for infrastructure improvement shall henceforth be redirected to Project Julian Recalibration, Phase I: Public Alignment Initiative."

The room was silent but for the scratching of the Quills. Lucilla was first to regain her voice.

"Does anyone on this Subcommittee know what Project Julian Recalibration entails?"

Veturius gave a smile so slippery it should have come with a warning. "It is, as stated, a matter of Public Alignment. All citizens are expected to align."

"Align with what?"

He spread his hands, palms up, as if to say: with the prevailing wind, or whatever passes for it. "Caesar's Vision."

Lucilla tried, not for the first time, to will the other senators into action by force of personality. None responded. Even the pigeon appeared to shrug.

"So," she said, "the city will go dry while Caesar aligns the populace?"

"Only temporarily," said Veturius. "The alignment will be more efficient, once the populace is motivated by thirst."

A muffled cough from the dais signalled that even Piso found this a stretch.

Lucilla gathered her materials. "If the Committee cannot explain the details of the project, I move for a ten-minute recess, to allow for the review of the associated documentation."

Veturius checked his own wrist, where a sundial would have left a mark, then said, "We are on recess until the water clock says so." He motioned for the

Quills, who retreated to the corridor, taking the scroll with them.

Lucilla sat in the sudden hush, feeling the damp weight of impending disaster settle around her. She stared at the frieze above the dais, at the aqueduct and the demigods, and wondered which was the more impressive fiction.

The silence did not last. The Quills reappeared, bearing a rolled document so enormous that it required all three to manoeuvre it through the doorway. They unfurled it with the precision of men unrolling a highway across enemy territory. The scroll revealed a flowchart so complex it could only have been designed by a committee desperate to avoid blame. At the apex, in letters the size of a child's fist: "JULIAN RECALIBRATION – PHASE I."

"Read," said Veturius, his voice bright with self-congratulation.

Quill #2 began: "Public Alignment Initiative is a city-wide effort to synchronise all civic, religious, and social activities with the New Calendar as promulgated by the Office of Time. Activities include, but are not limited to, the following: citizen assemblies, group recitations, and the ceremonial re-tuning of public clocks."

Lucilla glanced at the assembly. No one else looked confused, because confusion would have required an investment in the process.

She said, "None of this requires the diversion of aqueduct repair funds."

Veturius beamed. "It does if you read the fine print."

Quill #1, ever obliging, read: "All projects listed in

Subsection B must demonstrate compatibility with the Alignment Initiative. Aqueduct repairs are subject to review and, if necessary, delay until their impact on the public mood can be determined."

Lucilla closed her eyes. The urge to scream was so intense she feared her jaw would lock.

She reopened them. "May I see the original budget proposal for the Marcia repairs?"

Veturius was ready. "The master budget is currently under audit. We expect to have a redacted version available for review at the next full session."

Lucilla, careful not to break the pen in her hand, wrote: "Denied access. Reason: imperial confidentiality."

Veturius continued, "Of course, if you wish to file a motion, you may do so—"

"—in triplicate, via the Office of Official Histories," Lucilla finished for him. "I'm familiar with the process."

Chairman Piso blinked, then said, "Shall we proceed to the next item?"

Lucilla gathered her scrolls, wrapped them tightly enough to blanch her knuckles, and rose from her seat. "No further business," she said, voice calm but dangerously so. "I'll be in the archives, recalibrating the public mood."

As she turned to go, Quill #3 piped up—perhaps programmed for thoroughness. "There is also, Senator, an annex about the festival schedule. It says here that the Ides of March is to be repurposed, culturally. Something about new branding."

Lucilla stopped. "The Ides?"

"Yes," said Quill #3. "It's to be recast as a Day of

National Renewal. Complete with revised rituals and a parade."

The pigeon, perhaps catching the tension, flapped down and landed on the edge of the scroll. It pecked at the word "Renewal," then shat directly onto "Parade."

Lucilla's eyes narrowed to the width of a conspiracy. "Thank you," she said. "You've been most illuminating."

She departed, her mind already outlining the next step, her hands still white around the evidence.

Behind her, the subcommittee returned to form, Chairman Piso resuming the day's nap as if it had never been interrupted, Veturius humming to himself in a minor key. The Quills, their task complete, rerolled the scroll and filed it away in the gap where common sense had once resided.

In the hall, Lucilla paused to catch her breath, then strode away, the force of her passage scattering a pair of junior clerks and their documentation. She did not notice. She was already planning her revenge.

The walk to the Temple of Janus was brief, but it offered Lucilla Minor sufficient time to calibrate her next betrayal. The street ran uphill and, as a matter of city planning or divine spite, was perpetually under repair. She traversed it at a pace designed to intimidate, pausing only to sidestep a crew of municipal diggers, who appeared to be excavating the same flagstone they had, by her count, replaced six times in as many months. At the summit, she found the temple's front doors chained and sported a hand-lettered placard: "Closed for Calendar Maintenance – Consult Rear Entrance."

Lucilla did not sigh. She regarded the sign as one might a particularly inept lie, then circled to the back, past the bins overflowing with worn-out calendar tablets and the spent bottles of ceremonial wine. The rear door, as always, was unlocked and unguarded. She stepped through, into the cool blue dim of the antechamber, and found herself confronted by silence—unusual, for an institution that prided itself on hourly chimes.

The archive annex occupied a windowless quadrant of the ground floor. Its custodians, a breed of civil servant immune to boredom and light, worked in a warren of aisles so tight that two archivists could not pass without one of them declaiming an apology in perfect Ciceronian. Lucilla navigated the corridor by memory, pausing at the "Staff Only" sign and then ignoring it.

She found Gellia, the temple's Senior Archivist, at her customary station: hunched over a desk the size of a funeral barge, cross-referencing calendar decrees with what appeared to be a copy of the city's birth records. Gellia had once been Lucilla's confederate in a doomed campaign to rationalise the public holidays, and though her hair was now as white as the wax on her desk, her posture and mood were unchanged.

"Lucilla Minor," she said, without looking up. "To what does the temple owe the discomfort?"

"Do you have a current copy of the Project Julian Recalibration proposal?"

"Several. Would you like it alphabetically, by date, or in the original incompetence?"

"Surprise me."

Gellia set down her stylus, wiped her fingers on a handkerchief, and rose from the desk with the stately awkwardness of a tortoise promoted to higher office. She led Lucilla deeper into the annex, past walls lined with scrolls, tablets, and more experimental forms of time-keeping than the human mind was meant to contemplate. They paused at a door labelled "Transition Edicts – Pending."

Inside, dust spiralled through shafts of afternoon light. Three apprentice acolytes argued in whispers over a heap of mismatched festival schedules. Gellia snapped her fingers, and they scattered, leaving behind only the perfume of cheap ink and the echo of a bicker over leap days.

Gellia reached to a high shelf and withdrew a scroll double-sealed in black and imperial blue. She caressed the wax with something like reverence, then handed it to Lucilla. "If you open it, you have to read it aloud. Tradition."

Lucilla cracked the seal. The first line, rendered in a calligraphy so ornate it practically bled anxiety, read:

"The Ides of March to be observed as a Day of Renewal and Solemn Applause, in perpetuity, by decree of Caesar and the Council of Temporal Harmony."

She read the next lines, her voice steady but losing altitude with each sentence:

"The following schedule is to be enacted:

(1) *At the sixth hour, all citizens to attend their local forum for the recitation of oaths;*

(2) *At the seventh hour, a public parade in the name of Social Unity;*

(3) *At the eighth hour, renewal of all legal contracts, debts, and personal allegiances;*

(4) *At the ninth hour, mass recalibration of the civic calendar, with new editions to be distributed henceforth, commencing from the date of Caesar's birth."*

Lucilla set the scroll on the desk. The air, she noticed, had grown colder.

"Do you see?" said Gellia, voice pitched just above a whisper. "They're not just changing the holidays. They're rewriting the history of time."

Lucilla's hands found each other and locked tight. "Does anyone else know?"

Gellia shrugged. "The acolytes suspect. The Quills will have heard it by now. But you're the first senator to show up in person. The rest prefer to leak their outrage in private. To the archives, or to their wives."

Lucilla rolled the scroll closed. "May I have a copy?"

Gellia grinned, not unkindly. "I thought you'd never ask." She reached into her sleeve and drew out a waxed slip, already prepared, as if this moment had always been scheduled.

Lucilla took it. "This could be dangerous for you."

Gellia looked to the shaft of dying light on the floor. "I spent thirty years archiving the holidays Rome tried to forget. I would rather be remembered for leaking one than cataloguing the rest."

Lucilla smiled, a flicker only, then let it drop. "I won't mention your name."

"Please do," said Gellia, voice rising as the acolytes reassembled in the hall, their argument about solstice rites now punctuated by laughter. "It'll give the next archivist something to live up to."

Lucilla turned to leave, but the archivist's voice caught her.

"If you leak it, they'll call it pre-emptive treason. They're already drafting the guidelines. Don't get caught."

Lucilla paused at the threshold. "Then they'd better update the charges. Because I intend to leak it twice."

She left the annex, the slip tight in her fist, and did not allow herself to tremble until she was safely out of sight.

NINE

Decimus Flaccus arrived at the Forum at the hour between the market's second collapse and the first gathering of the philosophers, when the morning's incidents had just begun to ferment into legend. The air was heavy, like a thick slurry of citrus peel, roasted chickpea, and the industrial reek of fresh whitewash applied to statues whose heads were already due for recall. He waded through a corridor of hawkers, their cries overlapping like sparrows at a sacrificial feast, each promising their wares would last longer than the next administration. Underfoot, the paving stones sweated out the previous night's fog in a manner that left every third step uncertain, and, above, the birds practiced a form of aerial jurisprudence on anyone insufficiently shielded by hair or rank.

He kept his head down, eyes bleary from a sleepless night spent rehearsing plausible deniabilities, hands locked to the scroll case that had become, in the last twelve hours, both his shield and his curse. His progress was checked at intervals by minor collisions—an old woman with a basket of defective augury eggs, a runner distributing handbills for an "improved" calendar, two small children engaged in a contest to see who could insert more gravel into the exposed toes of passing strangers.

At the centre of the Forum, where the official and unofficial news converged in a whirlpool of contradiction, Decimus encountered his first omen: a crowd, not of the usual loiterers or petitioners, but of men and women clustered around a rickety market stall draped in a banner reading "THE TRUE PROPHECY—FOR A FAIR DENARIUS." The stall itself was a masterpiece of improvisation: its planks nailed at haphazard intervals, a wash of blue pigment running down from the sign to stain the vendor's arms, and a precarious display of scrolls arranged like a barricade against sense.

The vendor, a man of such indeterminate parentage that his nose alone seemed to have outlived three dynasties, looked up as Decimus approached. His eyes were yellow with enterprise; his smile, a rack of bets lost and paid for in teeth.

"Flaccus, is it?" he said, not waiting for confirmation. "Come to see your words in action?" He spread his hands to encompass the mob, which was now surging and eddying as fresh arrivals elbowed in to inspect the latest edition.

Decimus blinked, once, then twice, certain that sleep deprivation was playing some cruel trick on the optic nerve. But no—his own handwriting, or at least a deft forgery, stared back at him from the topmost scroll:

"Beware the man with cheekbones like thunder / For he shall tear the state asunder."

He mouthed the line in silence. It was not his, not in form, but the cadence was right, the threat unmistakable.

The vendor grinned. "We fixed the pacing," he said. "The old version was too long in the middle. Also, this way it rhymes."

Decimus felt the chill of panic, precise as a dropped scalpel. "Where did you get this?" he asked, voice more air than tone.

"From the gods, obviously." The vendor winked, then, seeing that Decimus was not amused, added, "Or maybe from Hortensius. He said you'd want the best copy. It's authentic, see? Red thread, double wax, water-marked with the Temple of Apollo's seal—genuine, except for the bits I fixed."

A hand snaked out of the crowd and seized the nearest scroll. Its owner, a woman with the biceps of a professional grain-hauler, read aloud with a stage voice built for the amphitheatre:

"Beware the man with cheekbones like thunder—"

"—for he shall tear the state asunder!" the crowd finished, with a kind of delighted horror.

Decimus tried to insert himself between two large men who smelled of salt fish and public urinals, but the vendor held up a finger. "There's more," he said, and produced a second scroll, this one stamped "REVISED— NOW WITH ENDING."

"Let me see that," said Decimus, but the vendor was already unrolling it for the benefit of the mob.

"'The day Rome changes will begin with a bray /

And the state will be ruled by the Ass who delays.'" He chuckled. "The crowd loves that bit. They think it's about the Consul, but who can say?"

The phrase was picked up, amplified, mangled in the retelling until, by the time it reached the back of the mob, it was being chanted by a clutch of students, one of whom had already adapted it into a song with gestures that left little to the imagination.

Decimus's hands, clammy with desperation, scrabbled at his satchel for the original prophecy, the one he had intended to destroy but now carried everywhere like a charm against disaster. He scanned the crowd for Hortensius and found him, as predicted, loitering near the fountain, wine-skin in hand and a smile that could only be described as criminally relaxed.

Hortensius caught his gaze and raised his skin in a toast. "You're a prophet now, Flaccus! You made the scrolls, the scrolls made the legend, and now"—he gestured at the mayhem—"the legend will make history, whether you want it or not."

Decimus fought his way clear of the mob and approached the fountain, which bubbled with the suspicious murkiness of a public utility recently downgraded to "optional." Hortensius, for his part, leaned against the basin as if it were the threshold of his own mausoleum.

"What have you done?" Decimus hissed, low and urgent. "This was supposed to be a joke—a rumour. Now it's—"

"—Rome's favourite bedtime story," said Hortensius, with the unhurried confidence of a man who had long since decided that consequences were for other people.

"And you should see the variants. There's one about the donkey that's so popular, I hear the donkey will be getting its own feast day."

Decimus massaged his temples, which throbbed in time with the chant echoing across the Forum. "They'll want to know who wrote it," he said, mostly to himself.

"Everyone already knows," said Hortensius. "I told them it was you. Who else has the cheekbones?"

Decimus was prepared to retort, but a sudden commotion interrupted them. Down the main steps of the Curia came a cohort of city clerks in full regalia, led by none other than Tribune Scaevola, his toga resplendent in the new-season off-white and his face bearing the expression of a man who had just been informed, in writing, that his favourite statute was about to be repealed.

"Make way for the Tribune!" shouted one of the clerks, but the crowd, already high on prophecy, made only token efforts to part. Instead, the chant intensified:

"Cheekbones like thunder—cheekbones like thunder—"

Decimus tried to melt into the background, but it was already too late. The eyes of the mob had fixed on him, and, in that instant, he understood how easy it was for a scribe to become a scapegoat. He backed away, only to collide with the market stall, which, under the collective weight of prophecy and poor carpentry, collapsed in a glorious cascade of scrolls, pamphlets, and one unfortunate roasted fowl that had served as the vendor's lunch.

Hortensius, never one to miss an exit, sidestepped the wreckage and clapped Decimus on the shoulder. "If I were you, I'd buy up the rest before the price goes up.

Or"—he lowered his voice—"burn them all and hope you're not too late."

Decimus, propelled by a mixture of fear and inertia, began scooping up armfuls of the scrolls, shoving coins at the vendor (who accepted them with the mournful dignity of a man mugged by fate). He bundled the scrolls into his satchel, only to notice, with a rising sense of despair, that a teenager with ink-stained fingers had already set up a copy station on the other side of the square and was cranking out fresh editions at a rate that would have shamed a swarm of locusts.

The noise grew: "Beware the man with cheekbones like thunder—"

A voice cut across the tumult, shrill and undeniable. "Silence!" it commanded, and for a moment, Rome obeyed.

At the edge of the steps stood Licinia, her hair wild as the city's future, her robes billowing in the sudden wind as if she had conjured the weather from nothing. She raised her arms, palms outstretched, and the crowd, hungry for spectacle, fell into a hush.

"The gods have spoken!" she intoned, voice rising and falling in the practiced cadence of the inspired and the slightly mad. "The prophecy is not a warning, but a charge! You"—here she stabbed a finger at Decimus—" have been chosen!"

A ripple of excitement passed through the mob, followed by a round of applause, then a volley of nuts and fruit thrown in the general direction of the Tribune.

Licinia descended the steps with the confidence of someone who had never been told "no." She reached the fountain, where Decimus stood paralysed, and seized his hand in both of hers. "Be proud," she said, ignoring his attempts at protest. "Few are selected to make history with their words. Fewer still survive the making."

"I didn't write the thunder bit," Decimus managed.

"It doesn't matter," said Licinia, with the certainty of a woman who had, on occasion, communed with walls. "Truth is what is repeated. And today, the city repeats you."

She released him, then, with a theatrical whirl, turned to address the Forum. "Look!" she declared, pointing to the far end, where a donkey had, through no fault of its own, positioned itself squarely in the main thoroughfare. At its feet, a discarded copy of the prophecy flapped in the breeze; the donkey, recognising destiny when it saw it, commenced to chew the scroll with the air of a connoisseur.

A child cried out, "The donkey reads the future!" and, within seconds, the animal was surrounded by a semi-religious procession of street urchins, failed augurs, and a troupe of itinerant philosophers, all of whom had chosen to interpret the event in ways that best suited their next meal.

Hortensius sidled up to Decimus, wine-skin now empty, and whispered, "I told you, they'd love the donkey. If the prophecy had mentioned you, you'd be drawing straws for your own execution."

On the steps, the Tribune had finally located his voice. "This is an unofficial assembly!" he bellowed. "Cease and disperse, or be subject to fine and censure!"

Licinia ignored him, launching into an impromptu

interpretive dance that was either the sacred rite of the God of Delays or a tribute to all the appointments she had ever missed. The crowd followed suit, swaying in rhythm, chanting the revised prophecy with increasing fervour.

Decimus, battered by the collision of fate, bureaucracy, and spectacle, did what any self-respecting Roman would do: he slumped against the nearest column and waited for the worst to pass.

But the worst, as always, was only beginning. The wind, picking up the discarded scrolls, carried them into the fountain, where they dissolved into a floating bloom of red and blue ink. The vendor, seeing his stock evaporate, began to auction the remaining scrolls at five times the original price, while the copyist, sensing a business opportunity, recruited two additional apprentices and tripled production.

Licinia's dance had reached a climax. She spun, arms raised, and declared, "The God of Delays speaks! All matters must now wait until the donkey leaves the Forum!"

The mob, delighted, took up the refrain. "All matters wait! All matters wait!"

At the far end of the square, Tribune Scaevola's parade faltered, then disintegrated, as the clerks, unable to out-shout the crowd, resorted to shoving their paperwork into satchels and making a tactical retreat.

The donkey, unmoved, continued its meal.

Decimus, watching as the city surrendered to the rhythm of its own farce, understood that the prophecy, once a clever lie, had become a self-fulfilling truth. He looked at his hands, now stained with ink and citrus, and wondered whether, in another life, he might have preferred the fate of the donkey.

Hortensius, reading his thoughts, raised a toast with the last dregs of his wine-skin. "To survival," he said. "History's only true reward."

Above, the pigeons circled, dropping their own footnotes to the day's events. The air vibrated with the overlapping hymns of rumour and revision, each rewriting the last. And in the chaos, Decimus felt himself recede, not into oblivion, but into the footnote at the bottom of the page—the place where, for better or worse, history would remember him.

The alley behind the Temple of Concord was one of those rare spaces in Rome that seemed to exist for no other reason than to allow the city to exhale. Here, the noise of the Forum decayed into a tired hush, and even the midday sun, after its brutal conquest of the main avenues, slouched off to rest in the crook of a crooked roof. Decimus Flaccus, face streaked with the residue of other people's lunches and his own near-misses, ducked into the passage with the desperation of a man seeking sanctuary and knowing, even as he entered, that such a thing no longer existed.

The first impression was of laundry. Every level of the buildings, from basement hovel to garret, was hung with bedsheets and undergarments, each limp in the stagnant air, forming a soft maze of swaying corridors. He brushed past a row of tunics, startling a spider the size of a denarius, and paused to catch his breath. The wall opposite was a palimpsest of failed graffiti, election slogans overwritten by curses, curses buried beneath crude illustrations of exactly what most citizens thought of their Senate.

High above, a cat the colour of unripe olives glared down from a second-storey sill, tail twitching with legislative disdain. Decimus stared back, lost the contest, and sagged onto a crate that, by the smell and the imprint of its previous user, had recently hosted a family of pickled herring.

He did not hear Domitia approach. He only became aware of her when she stepped from behind a freshly laundered sheet, the damp fabric billowing around her with a studied indifference to drama.

She did not speak. Instead, she regarded him with the expression of someone asked to fix a problem she had not caused, but would, for the right price, be willing to make worse.

Decimus started, nearly losing his balance on the crate. "How—? I didn't see you."

"That's the point," said Domitia. She moved to stand in the thin triangle of shadow beside him, her eyes flickering over his face, the stains on his clothes, the satchel clutched in both hands. "You've had an interesting morning."

He tried for dignity, failed, and attempted a joke instead. "If you're selling better fortunes, I'd like to buy one in advance."

Domitia's gaze, already sharp, refined itself into a blade. "Before this morning, you went to the Temple of Janus. You met with an ex-augur and a man who cannot stop losing his job. Yesterday, you left the Archives carrying something you didn't check out, and today you tried to buy up the entire city's supply of a scroll no one was supposed to read. Now you're hiding in an alley that does not, technically, appear on any public map."

He opened his mouth, closed it, then opened it again. "I have a difficult job," he said. "Most days it involves running in circles, but today—"

"Today you're being watched," Domitia interrupted. "By me, at the moment. Later, by others. Some are better at it than I am."

He tried to scan the alley, but the press of linen and the stillness of the air made the world seem flat and depthless.

Domitia stepped closer, so close he could smell the lye on her hands, the lemon oil on her wrist, the faint coppery tang that marked her as a woman who dealt with blood as often as with stains. She tilted her head, an affectation that might have been flirtation if not for the deliberate way she blocked his only path to escape.

"Was it your idea to start the rumour?" she asked. "Or was that the archivist's?"

"I—" He hesitated. "It was a joke. At first. Hortensius said—"

"He says a lot of things," Domitia said. She plucked a thread from her sleeve and let it fall between them. "But this wasn't a joke. Not to the men who are now reassigning half the city guard to protect a donkey, or to the augurs who haven't slept since yesterday. Someone is very interested in who wrote the prophecy."

"I didn't write the rhyme, I didn't write any of it," Decimus insisted. "They made it up, assigned it to me—added the part about the cheekbones—"

Domitia blinked. "You're lying badly, Flaccus. You talk like a guilty man. And I've known many." She let the accusation settle, then sat on the crate next to him, not so much as glancing to check its hygiene.

For a moment, neither spoke. The cat above resumed its study of events, now joined by two children who peered out from behind a third-floor railing, chewing on figs and the possibility of watching a public disgrace in progress.

Domitia spoke softly. "There's a group—call them a club, or a conspiracy, or a very persistent debating society —who think the only way to save Rome is to knock it sideways. They want the prophecy to be true. They want you to be their prophet."

"Then they're going to be disappointed," said Decimus. "I have no interest in overthrowing anything. I just want my old life back."

Domitia's mouth twisted, a smile not quite achieved. "You can't unsqueeze the grape, Flaccus. All you can do is decide whether you're going to drown, or ferment."

He considered, then glanced down the length of the alley, hoping for a distraction. A child's ball bounced against a wall, then rolled to a stop at his feet. He picked it up, tossed it back, and watched as the child's mother, a figure of imposing bulk, appeared at the end of the alley to retrieve her offspring. The mother's eyes met Domitia's for a half-second, a tiny nod exchanged, and then she was gone. Decimus shivered, unsure whether he had just been saved or identified for later disposal.

Domitia leaned in, lowering her voice. "You need to leave the city," she said. "But you won't. Which means you have to choose—let the prophecy eat you, or use it."

He looked at her, trying to divine which answer she wanted.

She saved him the trouble. "I can help. But only if you tell me everything. No edits, no footnotes."

He swallowed. "And if I say no?"

Domitia stood, dusted off her hands. "Then you'll be the city's next cautionary tale. They'll write a new rhyme about you, and it won't even scan."

He found himself nodding, a reflex learned from years of dealing with people who never really left a room until they had what they wanted. "What now?"

She shrugged. "Meet me at the west gate, just after sundown. Come alone. Bring any scrolls you haven't managed to destroy." She paused, looked him over, and added, "And if you see the donkey again, follow it."

Before he could protest, she was gone—absorbed into the alley as if the laundry had simply reabsorbed her presence. The only trace she left was a faint warmth on the crate and, hanging in the air, a scent equal parts lemon and inevitability.

Decimus sat for a moment, staring at the blank wall opposite. Above, the cat yawned, stretched, and turned its back, as if pronouncing a final judgement.

He rose, dusted off his toga, and prepared to return to the city's surface. Already, the distant sounds of the

Forum reached him: the chant of cheekbones, the bray of a donkey, the slow, grinding tick of a government not yet aware of its own obsolescence.

He took a step forward, then stopped, checking the sky for omens. It was empty, as ever, except for a laundry line strung between the houses. There, in the breeze, a sheet snapped open and closed, like the wings of a pigeon, or the shutters on a cell.

He took it as a sign, of something, and followed the alley back to its uncertain conclusion.

TEN

He found the address precisely where Domitia's note had indicated: a nondescript doorway at the foot of a five-storey Subura tenement, wedged between a cabbage vendor and a shop whose window displayed nothing but dust and the fading dreams of its owner. The door itself was unmarked, except for the faint brownish patch at knuckle height—either the residue of a thousand supplicants or evidence that the landlord had given up on cleaning anything, ever.

He knocked, as instructed, three times and then once more, which he hoped would signal both obedience and a healthy respect for improvisation. The door opened with the resigned exhalation of hinges that remembered better centuries. He was greeted by a boy of indeterminate age and allegiance, who sniffed, checked the satchel, and then jerked his chin inwards.

Down a corridor that grew darker, narrower, and clammier with each step, past a row of barrels leaking wine and, from the sound of things, ongoing familial disputes, then down a set of stairs whose treads had been individually modified by history's least efficient carpenter. The walls here sweated in time to the heartbeat of the city. At the base, a sconce burned low and unsteady. A painted arrow, so hastily applied that the plaster still bubbled, pointed left.

He followed. The passage opened onto a cellar so crowded with bodies and animal presence that for a moment he thought he had stumbled upon a livestock auction disguised as a religious rite. The smell was what struck him first: the unholy mixture of wine, incense, sweat, and cheese. Then the sound—a low, pulsing mutter that ran beneath the more ceremonial noises like a tributary of dissent.

At the centre of the room stood Licinia, barefoot, robes wine-stained and clinging. She projected the easy gravity of someone who had spent a lifetime in spaces with inadequate ventilation, and now drew her power from the lack of it. She stood behind a makeshift altar—an upended wine barrel, draped with what appeared to be an old bedsheet and a mat of vine leaves. Her face, always more geometry than expression, split into a precise smile at his arrival.

"Flaccus!" she called, voice ringing clear and cold as the amphorae lining the back wall. "You are exactly on time, which is to say, fatefully late."

He crossed the threshold, careful to avoid the perimeter where a circle of chalk and spilled grain marked the ritual boundary. In this way, the superstitious and the practical among her followers were both appeased.

She beckoned. The crowd—a mixture of wine merchants, debtors, professional mourners and at least one man who had been permanently banned from the public baths—turned as one to assess the new arrival. A donkey, roped to a support pillar, observed proceedings with the steady intelligence that only comes from a lifetime of waiting for things to pass.

Licinia extended a hand, palm up. "You brought the scroll?"

He unfastened the satchel, drew out the parchment, and placed it on her open palm. She cradled it as one might a dangerous bird: with simultaneous reverence and expectation of being bitten. She held it up to the torchlight, rotated it, and then pressed it to her forehead.

"I feel its weight," she intoned, "and also its utter lack of subtlety." She lowered the scroll, eyes twinkling. "Whoever composed this did not care for omens so much as for headlines."

A ripple of laughter, genuine or otherwise, passed through her acolytes. Decimus, sensing his role as participant rather than audience, awaited instruction.

Licinia gestured to a young woman in a tunic the shade of mildew; the girl stepped forward, brandishing a battered lyre. "Let us begin the clarification," Licinia said, which Decimus understood to mean: the ritual, as advertised.

The cultists arranged themselves in a loose semicircle, some kneeling, some standing with arms folded. One of them, a gaunt man wearing a child's scarf as a stole, set about arranging a tray of offerings—cheese rind, candied figs, a cluster of wilted spring onions, and, for reasons lost to protocol, an apple with a single bite removed. At the edge of the circle, the goat, ancient and flecked with pink powder, blinked in the candlelight.

Licinia raised her arms, and the room—by inclination or by cue—fell silent. "We gather," she began, "to interpret that which refuses interpretation. To pierce the veils not just of the future, but of the very bureaucracy that defines us. To mock the gods, and thereby honour them."

She motioned to the girl, who began plucking the lyre with a discordant earnestness. The donkey, perhaps insulted by the lack of musicality, brayed once, then settled back into impassivity.

Decimus knelt, as was expected, though the floor was neither clean nor accommodating. He noted the pattern of stains beneath the altar: concentric rings of wine, interspersed with smaller, sharper outlines where candles had guttered out and left little cairns of wax.

Licinia produced a cup—a communal one, by the look of it—and filled it from a jug that sloshed as if carrying both liquid and history. She drank, then passed the cup round the circle. Each cultist took a sip, some reverently, some with the faces of men who had never acquired a taste for this particular sacrament.

When the cup reached Decimus, he hesitated, then drank. The taste was resinous, sour, and left a slick on his teeth that felt both ancient and newly alive.

"Tonight," said Licinia, "we ask the old question.

Who is the author of fate: the scribe, or the hand that guides it?"

She looked directly at Decimus, as if expecting him to answer.

He said, "It depends whether the hand is paid by the line, or by the outcome."

A laugh, this time more genuine, circled the room.

Licinia nodded, acknowledging both wit and truth. "We have here a prophecy," she said, unrolling the scroll and letting it unfurl over the wine barrel. "Not from the usual channels. Not sanctioned, not stamped, not even properly redacted. It names no names, but everyone knows who it means."

She read aloud:

"When the city's heart forgets to beat,
and augurs fight for scraps of truth,
the scribe will bleed the first account
and history will chew the rest."

She let the words settle, then rolled them back up. "It's not the worst prediction I've heard tonight," she said. "But it lacks conviction. It wants to be a warning, but ends as a resignation."

She set the scroll down and gestured for the goat, which was guided forward by the scarfed acolyte. The goat eyed Decimus with an intelligence that bordered on prosecutorial.

Licinia addressed the goat. "Well, Consul? Shall we read the future in your entrails, or is your opinion less metaphorical?"

Someone in the crowd giggled, and another muttered, "It's less painful than last week's attempt."

Licinia drew from her sleeve a handful of figs and offered one to the goat, which accepted it with a mixture of suspicion and greed. "Let this stand for the bloodless sacrifice," she said. "Let us interpret the prophecy in the spirit of the age: lazy, distracted, and above all, plausible."

She poured another round, this time into individual cups distributed by the acolytes. Decimus received his with the gratitude of a drowning man offered a less polluted stretch of river.

Licinia returned to the scroll, but now read from the reverse, where someone—probably Hortensius, Decimus thought—had scribbled a series of annotations in marginalia:

"Look to the ass, not the augur. The city's fate will ride a bray."

She raised an eyebrow. "The gods are feeling literal tonight."

The donkey, sensing its cue, gave a short, derisive snort.

Licinia set her cup aside, then perched herself on the barrel, feet dangling, arms draped along her knees. She fixed Decimus with a look that, for the first time, carried no theatrics.

"You came here with a question," she said.

He nodded.

"Ask it, but do not name yourself."

He hesitated, then spoke: "If a man is made the instrument of his own undoing, does the city blame the hand, or the music?"

Licinia considered. "Rome blames the conductor, then hires him to rewrite the next score." She leaned closer. "But if you are the scribe, you may yet choose the ending. That is the only power left to men like us."

He said, "What if the ending is already written?"

She smiled, a small and tired smile. "Then you improvise. You make the gods laugh, and the city forgets to bleed."

A clatter from the rear: the boy who had ushered him in was now attempting to corral a tray of biscuits through a crowd not interested in sharing. The biscuits arrived, broken and crumbling, but were accepted by the assembly as if they were a delicacy reserved for the gods themselves.

Licinia clapped her hands. "Let us conclude, before the fumes turn us all into philosophers."

The lyre girl struck a final, discordant chord. The cultists joined hands. The donkey brayed, the goat burped, and someone in the back attempted a recitation of dirty limericks in lieu of a closing prayer.

Licinia hopped down from the barrel and moved to Decimus's side. She leaned in, her breath sweet with wine and sharper purpose.

"Listen to me," she said, just for him. "You are not the author of this prophecy. You are its vessel. The city will pour its future through you, until you break or overflow. This is the way of Rome, and the reason why even our stones have memories."

He looked down, unsure whether to thank her or flee.

She pressed the scroll into his hand. "Take it," she said. "Burn it if you want. Eat it, even. It won't matter. The future's already set, but the footnotes are yours to write."

He gripped the scroll, and, for a moment, the world seemed to tilt, as if the city itself had exhaled in relief.

Then Licinia stood, gathered the remaining figs, and tossed them to the goat. "Go, now," she said. "Return to the Forum, or the archive, or wherever men like you are needed. And remember— it's not the end until the city says it is."

He backed out of the circle, past the acolytes, past the goat, past the donkey, which had managed to position itself squarely in front of the exit. He was forced to stroke its head before it would move aside. The donkey's ears flicked, as if in acknowledgement of a job well done.

In the corridor, the air was cool and almost clean. He climbed the stairs two at a time, bursting into the alley above like a man surfacing from a dream.

There, beneath the limp laundry and the indifferent moon, he saw her—Domitia, framed in the threshold, arms crossed, face unreadable.

He nodded, and she nodded back, and for a moment there was peace.

Then the city, never patient, resumed its noise, its business, and its perpetual, unquenchable appetite for stories.

He tucked the scroll into his toga, squared his shoulders, and stepped into the night, ready to edit the future, one footnote at a time.

The Tribune's office, like so many in the quarter, had not been designed for function. The room was a geometry of forced compromises: a desk too wide for the door, stacks of scrolls standing in for missing furniture, and a window whose shutter had long ago fused with its own paint. On the far wall, a mural of Justitia, faded to the colour of disappointment, glared down with the eyes scratched out —a legacy of the last riot, or possibly the one before. Tribune Scaevola spent most of his days in this room, cultivating the patience of a man who knew that, in Rome, the verdict always came after the appeal.

He sat with his back to the mural, arms folded, listening to the scritch of a quill as his junior clerk, a boy named Fabius, struggled to keep pace with the day's intake. The desk between them was a battleground: one side dominated by Scaevola's neat columns of parchment, the other a swamp of reports, sealed notes, and the detritus of a bureaucracy eating itself alive.

Scaevola regarded the most recent addition to his docket: a requisition for "ceremonial cutlery," filed under the innocuous heading of "Festival Supplies." The list included, among the usual parade of silver-plated spoons and sacrificial knives, a request for a dozen "double-edged daggers, standard military issue, preferably sharpened." He read this twice, then added it to the growing pile marked "Pretext for Insurrection."

Beside it, a wine-license infraction. A priestess, named only as "L.," cited for distributing home-fermented honey wine at a public gathering, in contravention of the current edict on state-approved spirits. The attached statement read: "Offender claims to have visions under the influence. Said visions included a goose, a man with cheekbones like thunder, and a city flooded with ink." Scaevola pencilled a note in the margin: "Assign to Omen Desk, Level II."

Next, a riot report from the Subura. The disturbance had started as an argument over the ownership of a singing bird and escalated into a street-wide brawl, with both sides citing a prophecy as justification for their conduct. The phrase repeated in the summary—"The knife returns to the hand that wrote it"—was familiar, even to Scaevola's sceptical ear. He clipped the report to the cutlery requisition, then stabbed a pushpin through both and mounted them on the board that occupied half the available wall.

The board was an artless web of twine, colour-coded wax, and faded receipts. Some saw in it the work of a paranoid; Scaevola considered it the only honest method of oversight. In the centre, a sliver of red string ran from the name "Flaccus, Decimus" to an ominous question mark. Around it, a spiral of escalating concern, from "Minor Fraud" to "Pre-coup Activity" to "Possible Divine Intervention."

Fabius, now sweating openly, shuffled the next scroll forward. "More omens, sir. They're coming in faster than we can file."

Scaevola took it, skimmed. "Another donkey sighting. This time, near the Marcelline baths. Was it reciting poetry?"

Fabius shrugged. "Witness said it 'seemed to know the city's business better than its own officials.' Then it ate a parade permit."

Scaevola grunted, tore the relevant segment, and affixed it beneath the previous donkey report. The number of sightings had doubled since yesterday. This was, in itself, not remarkable; Rome produced omens the way other cities produced cobblestones. What troubled Scaevola was the pattern: the donkey always appeared at moments of procedural collapse. A tribunal session cut short by a mass fainting; a grain shipment lost to "mysterious winds"; a scribe's suicide, note unsigned, but stamped with the wax of the Official Histories.

He examined the stringboard, eyes flicking from incident to incident, then leaned back, hands steepled. "They're not coincidences," he said. "They're test runs."

Fabius nodded as though this made sense, though his hand shook as he reached for the next scroll. "Another item, Tribune. This one's from the Forum. A scribe found dead, face—" He hesitated, then read, "—'arranged in a smile, the kind you'd see on a bad statue.'"

"Source?"

"A merchant. Also says a crowd gathered to hear a prophecy. The phrase is spreading, sir. They're calling it 'The New Word.'"

Scaevola closed his eyes, committed the data to his own internal stringboard. "Did the merchant sell anything at the scene?"

"Yes, sir. Copies of the prophecy."

He smiled, thin and sharp. "We're dealing with a viral event, then."

Fabius, to his credit, didn't ask what that meant. Instead, he set aside the scroll and began compiling the next batch.

Scaevola rose, crossing to the wall. He stood close enough to Justitia's ruined gaze to sense the disappointment. "The city's running ahead of schedule," he said. "If the augurs had any sense, they'd call the Ides now and be done with it."

He returned to the desk, selected a blank sheet, and began drafting a formal summons. "To: Senator Lucilla Minor, on account of her regrettable capacity for reason. Subject: Emergent Patterns in Festival Behaviour and Public Disturbance."

He paused, then added: "Bring all records of prior censures for reference. I suspect this will require more than one signature."

Fabius watched, silent, as Scaevola signed and sealed the note. When the Tribune looked up, the boy's face was pale.

"Is it that bad, sir?"

Scaevola considered, then shook his head. "No. It's worse. The city's inventing its own prophecy as it goes. We're already two disasters behind."

He gestured to the stringboard, the twine now crisscrossed with fresh lines. "We need to stop thinking like officials. We need to think like the men who'll write the next scroll."

Fabius nodded, determined now, and began to copy the summons in triplicate.

Scaevola turned again to the wall, tracing the line from "Flaccus, Decimus" to the latest riot, and from there to a circle marked "Unknown Entities." He stabbed a fresh pin into the spot.

"Find me the connection," he said, not really to Fabius, not really to himself. "There's always a pattern."

From outside, the noise of the city reached them: distant shouts, the clang of a parade being assembled, the steady rumble of rumour.

He returned to the desk, opened the next scroll, and waited for the city to reveal its next move.

It never took long.

ELEVEN

In the hours before the city surrendered to the furnace of midday, the alleyways adjoining the Forum grew crowded with the overflow of those too bored, too suspicious, or too disenfranchised to attend the official debates. In a shaded recess between a public latrine and the headquarters of a minor trade guild, a wooden crate had been set up as a stage, its sides still daubed with "This End Up" and a sequence of threatening arrows. The audience, arranged on amphorae and scavenged benches, regarded the assembly with a seriousness usually reserved for executions or free distributions of oil.

Atop the crate, an actor—he would have insisted on "tragedian," but had failed even the most basic test of theatre, which was to project without spitting—was declaiming to the world's smallest but most attentive mob. His toga, patched with strips of curtain, fluttered at every gesture; his hair, greased and combed forward, formed a sort of organic visor against the low sun. In his hands, the prophecy scroll—duplicated, annotated, and now heavily stage-directed—provided the script.

"Friends! Citizens! Seekers of truth!" the tragedian bellowed, pausing to fix the audience with a glare he believed to be withering. "Lend me your patience, for today the veil is ripped and the future, naked, parades before you!"

There was a ripple of laughter from the back. The tragedian ignored it, pivoting so his profile, sharp enough to skin a pomegranate, could be seen by all. "Beware! Beware! The city's fate is written not by the strong, nor the clever, nor the fox-faced sons of privilege! No, it is written—" he jabbed the scroll at the crowd "—by the man with cheekbones like thunder!" He paused, awaiting awe, but found only a soft, pained wheeze from the old man nearest the stage.

The audience, a mixture of youth in sashes, shop-keepers, and the odd pensioned soldier, exchanged glances. Some crossed themselves with the gestures of the recently converted, others made furtive notes on wax tablets. One woman, peeling a turnip with surgical effi-ciency, barely looked up.

A whisper travelled down the line of benches: "He's talking about the scribe, isn't he? The one from the archives?"

"Doesn't matter who. It's the cheekbones you have to watch," answered her neighbour.

Above them, the actor drew breath for the next onslaught. "And so it is written! When the Ides descend, and the city's pulse falters, beware the traitor-king, for his end shall come not from a blade, but from a tongue sharper than envy!"

He flung the scroll wide, the motion nearly toppling him. For a moment, balance and fate both teetered, then he caught himself and continued, voice growing shriller: "Let all Rome witness! Change, glorious change, is at hand! The Ass of Destiny brays; the soothsayers tremble; and at the last, a golden dawn led by one wise scribe shall restore our soul!"

This time, the crowd rumbled. Some cheered, some hissed, and a number merely blinked, unconvinced that their soul needed any such restoration.

At the alley's mouth, Domitia watched, half her face concealed by the shadow of a borrowed hood. She had chosen the spot for its sight lines, and because from here, she could see both the audience and the half-dozen figures trailing the crowd: a trio of bored city guards, two rival street preachers, and a man whose occupation was unclear but whose interest was absolute. She scanned the faces, the set of their mouths, the focus of their eyes—not on the tragedian, not really, but on the words. It was always the words that did the damage.

A child, selling sugared chickpeas from a tray, offered her a handful. She took two, weighed them, then tossed them at the tragedian's head. One bean bounced off his temple; he recoiled, found his place in the script, and picked up as if nothing had happened.

From down the lane, another presence approached: Lucilla Minor, hair pinned with the unyielding precision of a senatorial appointment, her gait betraying the limp of someone who had once run a marathon of bureaucracy and never quite recovered. She moved through the crowd with minimal displacement, but maximum efficiency, scanning for threats with the weariness of an auditor on the last day of audit season.

Domitia watched as Lucilla reached the front, arms folded, eyes narrowed to a thread. The tragedian, sensing an authority figure, redirected his invective toward her.

"And lo! The guardians of order, the stubborn, the old blood, stand in the way of destiny! But destiny is a river, madam, and it floods all banks!" He flourished the scroll, nearly losing his grip on the "river" metaphor.

Lucilla did not dignify him with a reply. Instead, she whispered to the turnip-peeling woman, "When did this start?"

"Yesterday, maybe the day before. They say it's real, that scroll."

"And do you believe it?"

The woman shrugged. "Doesn't matter if I do. Someone does, and they'll make it happen, just to prove themselves right."

Lucilla nodded, her expression tightening. "That's the problem with prophecy," she said. "It always seeks an editor."

The tragedian, now in the throes of his finale, shrieked, "Let all who hear take heed! The old ways are dead! The scribe is the new king! The city will bow to the one who writes its history—beware the cheekbones, and tremble!" He fell to his knees, arms spread, and the scroll rolled into the gutter.

There was applause, hesitant, then building as a few in the audience realised it might be watched or required.

The actor rose, bowed with grotesque solemnity, and was immediately mobbed by two street preachers demanding to see the scroll for themselves.

Domitia, seeing the conclusion, turned to leave, her interest already shifted to the murmured debates in the side street and the two men (definitely not of the theatre) quietly arguing over a sealed envelope marked "For the Archivist's Eyes Only." She slipped away, undetected, but not unremembered; several sets of eyes lingered on her retreating figure, then returned to the discussion at hand.

Lucilla remained in the front row, arms still folded, watching as the tragedian wiped sweat from his brow and the crowd dispersed into knots of rumour and speculation.

The turnip woman, having finished her snack, tapped Lucilla's knee. "You'll try to stop them?"

Lucilla shook her head. "Nothing stops a lie once it has an audience. Not in this city." She stood, glanced up at the strip of sky visible above the alley, then back to the departing crowd. "But someone has to document it. Otherwise, next week it will have a monument and a feast day."

A child, now emboldened by the end of the play, scooped the prophecy scroll from the gutter. He unrolled it, tried to read the ink, then shrugged and began to use it to swat at the pigeons.

Lucilla caught the tragedian by the elbow as he stepped off the stage. "Who gave you the script?" she asked, voice flat.

He hesitated, looked down at the ground, then up at

the guards now ambling closer. "No one. It was just there, in the open. Anyone could take it."

She nodded, released him. "They always can," she said, mostly to herself.

The tragedian, spooked, collected his script from the gutter and hurried off, his curtain-patched toga trailing mud. Lucilla watched until the alley was nearly empty, then walked the length of it, peering at the faces in every knot of conversation, listening for the next variant of the prophecy, the next embellishment or mutation.

When satisfied, or at least resigned, she turned back towards the Forum, her lips moving in a private tally of events. She did not notice the turnip woman following at a discreet distance, nor the guards who had decided, with typical pragmatism, to take a break before the next performance.

The alley, briefly transformed, returned to its usual state: a thoroughfare for waste and whispers, the air heavy with dust and the ghost of spectacle. A pigeon, missing half a toe, strutted onto the crate-stage and regarded the city with the indifferent majesty of one who knew that, in time, all history was written from the bottom up.

And, on the other side of the alley, behind a shuttered window, a hand copied down the lines of the prophecy, making small corrections and improvements, the future already mutating as it travelled.

TWELVE

The Baths of Agrippa, at the hour of Lucilla's arrival, were occupied by two classes of Roman: the professionally idle and the terminally oiled. The latter, glistening as though excreted rather than born, reclined on heated slabs of imported marble, engaging in the sacred rites of self-exposure and gossip. Here, among the mosaics depicting the more regrettable moments of myth, Lucilla Minor made her entrance, swaddled in a towel of such inadequate dimension that it suggested, to any observer, both a crisis and a statement.

Behind her trailed Decimus Flaccus, barefoot, half-draped in his own towel, and gripping the remains of his dignity with all the effectiveness of a man attempting to plug a dam with a fig. The tiled floor, slick with olive oil and the social ambitions of lesser men, offered no traction. He slipped once, then again, each time caught and steadied by Lucilla's grip on his elbow. That she used the opportunity to steer him as one might a recalcitrant goat was, by now, inevitable.

They passed through the central atrium—air thick with steam and the scent of overripe citrus—before making for the private alcoves that rimmed the caldarium. Each alcove, shielded from public view by a curtain or, in the grander suites, a slave, provided the powerful with a retreat from scrutiny, and the opportunity to re-enact the fall of Carthage in peace.

At the far end, behind a velvet rope that did not so much invite respect as repel bacteria, sat Caesar. He reclined, sculpturally nude, on a mound of woven linen, a plate of fruit within reach, and a single attendant at his feet, massaging what could only be described, even by the standards of the day, as an imperial ankle. A goblet of gold, brimming with wine, rested on his belly, the meniscus so calm it could have been a mirror.

Lucilla swept aside the rope with a motion that, in another context, would have merited censure. "Caesar," she said, voice measured but pitched to carry, "I apologise for the interruption. But the matter is urgent and, I fear, unfit for any protocol short of invasion."

Caesar, without looking up, flicked a piece of melon into his mouth. He chewed, swallowed, and gestured for her to continue. The attendant, eyes downcast, increased the intensity of the massage.

Decimus, mortified, attempted a bow, but succeeded only in rearranging his towel in a way that suggested both surrender and confusion.

Lucilla plunged ahead. "There is a plot against your person, and possibly against the institution of office itself. The specifics are... fluid, but the actors are numerous, the omens have aligned, and the date appears fixed."

Caesar raised an eyebrow, which, in the context of the bath, was the highest form of attention. "And the date?"

"The Ides," she said.

A beat. Then Caesar laughed—not the laugh of a man surprised or afraid, but of one who has just recalled an excellent joke and is about to tell it twice. He said, "If I had a denarius for every Ides, I'd have annexed Gaul twice over. What is it this time? A knife in the back, or the usual chicken liver in the water main?"

Lucilla did not flinch. "Both. And more. There is a prophecy—"

Here, Decimus interjected, voice quavering: "With respect, Caesar, it's not an official prophecy. More a—"

"—rumour," said Lucilla, "which, as you are aware, becomes prophecy when repeated by enough citizens."

Caesar fixed on Decimus. "You're the scribe. What does the record say?"

Decimus, who had been trying to absorb himself into the tilework, started. "That the Ides are traditionally considered... fraught. And that this year's calendar was, perhaps, optimistic in its scheduling."

The attendant, unbidden, produced a towel and began to mop Caesar's brow. Caesar allowed this, then dismissed the servant with a flick of his foot. He regarded Lucilla, then Decimus, then the fruit plate, which was now reduced to a rind and two grapes.

"So," said Caesar. "The Senate is concerned that I may not survive the month. Does the Senate intend to do anything about it, or is this to be a spectator sport?"

Lucilla said, "We recommend cancellation of all

public events through the Ides. Additional security. The recall of any personnel with ambiguous loyalties."

"Not the Games?" said Caesar, a grin starting in one corner of his mouth. "Surely you don't mean to deprive the city of its amusements. We only get one Ides a year."

Decimus, emboldened by the fact that his last attempt at speech had not led to execution, said, "Perhaps, if you reschedule the parade—move it forward, or delay it—"

"Delay it?" said Caesar, amused. "Do you know what happened the last time a public festival was delayed?"

"Flooding," said Lucilla, with the dryness of someone who had read the archives.

"Exactly," said Caesar. "The augurs have already promised good weather, and I intend to see if they can, for once, be correct."

He stood, stretching in a way that demonstrated, for all present, the reason why statues had been commissioned in his likeness. He strode to the edge of the alcove, towel slung over one shoulder, and regarded Lucilla as one might a promising but obstinate student.

"Senator Minor," he said, "I appreciate your concern. I do. The city would be poorer without your diligence. But Rome is founded on the principle that life is uncertain, and that one should meet it with a full stomach and, where possible, an empty bladder." He glanced at Decimus. "As for you, young scribe—if you are going to write a prophecy, do make it more entertaining. The last one was derivative."

Decimus, aghast, managed only, "I didn't— it wasn't mine— the authorship is disputed—"

"Everything is disputed in Rome," said Caesar. "That's why we have so many archives." He turned, dismissing them with a smile. "Now, if you'll excuse me, I must rehearse my speech for the Ides. There's a section about the virtues of humility which, frankly, I haven't mastered."

Lucilla, realising she had achieved exactly nothing, inclined her head. "As you wish, Caesar."

Decimus, relieved to still have his job and, more importantly, his head, bowed again, then slipped in a puddle and had to be helped upright by the departing attendant.

They retraced their steps, passing once more through the court of the oiled and the damned. In the corridor, Decimus whispered, "He's not going to do anything, is he?"

Lucilla said, "He's going to do exactly what Rome always does. Ignore the warning and schedule a celebration."

Decimus tried, and failed, to find solace in this. He wrapped his towel tighter and followed Lucilla into the steam, the laughter of the emperor echoing behind them, louder than any prophecy.

Decimus returned to the Office of Official Histories as the city's noise declined from riot to farce. The corridors, bright in the morning and sullen by dusk, now possessed the quiet of an emptied amphitheatre, the echo of departed crowds pressed flat by the gravity of unfinished work. The lamps, hung at intervals insufficient for either safety or style, flickered along the main archive hall, their light not so much illuminating as performing a hasty inventory of the dust.

He entered, as always, with the sensation of being observed. Every shelf had its own personality, its cubby-holes arranged in moods—some judgmental, others merely indifferent. The tables bore the detritus of a day's effort: open ledgers, scrolls in various states of collapse, a broken stylus preserved in a cup of stagnant water as though awaiting official burial. In the far corner, an office pigeon perched atop the wax-seal press, surveying the stacks with the proprietary arrogance that comes from being, in a technical sense, the highest authority in the room.

Decimus paused just inside the threshold. There was comfort in the familiarity, yes, but it was the comfort of an old wound, a pain that had outlasted its explanation.

He set to work. The evening's project was an act of reclamation: to bring the official record up to date, to catch the prophecy in its lies and footnote it into submission. He had prepared the forms in advance, three sets—one for the Library of Memory, one for the Ministry of Public Assurance, and a third for the office pigeon, which, as experience had taught him, served both as courier and informal quality control.

He arranged the papers, uncorked the ink, and set his pen to the first heading. The words that came, at first, were deliberate: *On the Events of the Present Ides, and the Widespread Circulation of Certain Rumours Thereof.*

He glanced up, feeling the pressure of scrutiny increase.

It was only then he noticed Hortensius, seated in a high-backed chair in the shadows, hands clasped over his belly and an air of expectant amusement.

"Working late," said Hortensius, without moving. "That's how it begins."

Decimus stifled the urge to glare. "I thought you'd resigned. Or been dismissed. Or—"

"All three," said Hortensius. "But the beauty of our profession is that it's impossible to fire a man whose absence makes more work than his incompetence."

Decimus continued writing, hoping that diligence might serve as both shield and weapon. "I'm updating the narrative. For the record. I intend to clarify that the prophecy is, in fact, a product of—"

"Boredom and a need for relevance," said Hortensius. "They'll love that." He leaned forward, the light catching the streak of ink across his cheek. "But it won't change the fact that the prophecy is now the official version. The more you argue with it, the more true it becomes."

Decimus signed the first copy and moved to the next. "That's not how records work," he said. "Accuracy is a function of—"

"Persuasion," said Hortensius. "You think the scrolls matter. But what matters is whose copy gets cited." He lifted a battered pamphlet from the floor and waved it, as if fanning a flame. "Look here: a poet in the Subura has already written a comedy based on your prophecy. There's a talking goat in Act Three. The goat wins. By tomorrow, they'll be putting on rehearsals in the Forum."

Decimus, who had spent his life believing in the slow accumulation of truth, felt a thread of panic. "If we lose control of the record—"

"Then we become history," said Hortensius. "And not the flattering kind."

He tossed the pamphlet onto the table, where it landed face-up. The title, rendered in a riot of exclamation points, read: *The Ides of Ass: A Tragedy in Five Acts* (*Two Survive*). Beneath it, an illustration of a donkey in a laurel wreath, winking.

Decimus covered the pamphlet with a sheaf of official forms and pressed down, as though suffocating a bad rumour. "If you have nothing useful to contribute—"

"Oh, but I do," said Hortensius. He produced a fig from his sleeve, bit into it, and spoke with his mouth full. "I'm here to witness your moment of fame. Or infamy. There's a rumour in the lower corridors that you've been selected for advancement. That the Ministry has noticed your gift for self-effacement. They want you to write the next official account—one that will please the gods, the Senate, and the very important new audience in the provinces. You're going to save Rome, Flaccus, one footnote at a time."

Decimus set his pen down, felt the weight of the day settle on his spine. "If that's true, it's because someone wants to make me the next casualty."

Hortensius smiled, lips wet with fruit. "Only if you do a bad job. Do a good one, and you'll be blamed for the aftermath instead."

He rose, the motion accompanied by a symphony of

creaks. He wandered to the nearest scroll rack, trailed his fingers along the spines, and selected a volume at random. "Remember," he said, "the only thing worse than an unreliable narrator is an expendable one."

A noise at the door—a sharp, metallic clack—heralded the arrival of a junior clerk, face pale with the burden of urgent news. The clerk approached, presented a wax-sealed envelope to Decimus, and waited, fidgeting, for instructions.

Decimus broke the seal. The document inside was short, and written in a hand so precise it could only have been forged by someone terrified of error.

By order of the Ministry of Moral Memory, you are hereby assigned to Narrative Containment and Emotional Clarification. All previous assignments are suspended. Immediate compliance is expected. Failure to comply will be interpreted as tacit support for the heretical version of events.

Decimus read it again. The words did not change.

Hortensius, peering over his shoulder, made a low whistle. "Congratulations. You're no longer an historian. You're a biographer of the present."

The office pigeon, sensing the conclusion of business, flapped down from its perch and strutted along the table, pecking at the crumbs of dried wax and ink. It fixed Decimus with a glassy, inscrutable stare.

Decimus gathered his things—forms, ink, the unfinished narrative—and rose, the legs of his chair scraping a dirge against the tile. He was halfway to the corridor before Hortensius called after him:

"Remember, Flaccus: the city's fate is always in the hands of men who think they're only holding a pen."

Decimus did not turn. He left the hall, footsteps echoing, as the archives resumed their silence, broken only by the pigeon's faint coo of judgment and the distant sound of Hortensius licking fig from his teeth.

THIRTEEN

Tribune Scaevola's office enjoyed the distinction of being, by some consensus, the most depressing chamber in the Tribunal complex. The light, never abundant in this wing, had been dimmed further by a decade's worth of institutional neglect, leaving only a pale, fungoid glow to illuminate the business of civic retribution. The walls, once a blameless off-white, had settled into the colour of dampened pearl; the ceiling, bowed by years of condensation and collapsing ambition, dripped intermittently into a series of strategically placed amphorae. These overflowed in rainy weather, which this season meant always. Along the back wall, shelves sagged under the accumulated wisdom of the city's legal system, a wisdom expressed primarily in scrolls bound with twine and resentment. The air was a contest between ink, mildew, and the faint undertone of boiled cabbage rising from the adjacent break room.

Scaevola inhabited this world like an apostate monk: his toga perfectly folded, hair precisely trimmed to the regulation minimum, every visible surface of his desk cleared of distraction save for the implements of his trade —a quill, a sand-glass, and the three-tiered stamp apparatus by which he reduced chaos to precedent. In the far corner, a bust of Lady Justice glared blindly at proceedings, its blindfold having slipped years ago to rest at a rakish, satirical angle. This detail troubled Scaevola less than the persistent chip on the statue's lower lip, which he considered a metaphor for the current state of affairs.

On this particular morning, Scaevola found himself in receipt of the third formal complaint in as many days regarding unauthorised dissemination of prophecies in the public sphere. The relevant document, a sheet of suspiciously high-grade parchment, accused several parties—none named, all implied—of "circumventing the established licensing procedures for divine communication, thereby undermining the sanctity of the city's predictive apparatus." It was signed, in a tremulous but legible hand, by the Chief Augur Emeritus, who added in a footnote: "If the Tribunal will not act, the Forum will."

Scaevola read the complaint twice, then a third time. He stared at it as if by sheer concentration he might distil the essence of its malice and thereby neutralise it. He set the quill to the form and, after a pause for rhetorical effect, wrote: *Noted and to be reviewed. Suggest enhanced oversight for all augurial activities pending Ides. Attach schedule.* He blotted the ink, initialled in triplicate, and filed the sheet in the folder marked "Religious Escalations, Pending." The folder bulged, as all things did in the records wing, with the weight of unresolved grievance.

The moment his hand left the document, the door

creaked open, and a Junior Clerk entered, the man's skin still damp from the outer humidity, his hair matted with the evident effects of a misplaced umbrella. He carried an armload of scrolls, each stamped in a different shade of municipal authority, and attempted a bow. Several scrolls took the opportunity to escape, spiralling to the floor where they unrolled themselves like accusatory tongues.

"Sir," the Junior Clerk managed, "urgent reports from the submarket, and an anonymous incident from the Temple of Janus. Also, a note for your personal attention." He extended the note, which trembled slightly in his grip, then bent to gather the scattered scrolls, his knees making a popping noise that implied either youth or mismanagement.

Scaevola accepted the note with a nod, not bothering to conceal his disappointment at the display of inefficiency. He scanned the page. "Anonymous, you say?"

"Yes, Tribune."

"Ink analysis?"

"Domestic batch, sir. Possibly from the scribal quarter off the Aventine. The scent—"

"I can smell it," Scaevola said, dry as the ink. "Next time, use gloves."

The Junior Clerk bobbed, then deposited the remaining scrolls in the 'Immediate' basket, which now overflowed in a way that suggested nothing in the city was ever truly deferred.

The note itself was succinct: "It has come to our attention that several boxes of ceremonial daggers, ordered for the Ides parade, have been intercepted and replaced with counterfeit props. The city's official supply is compromised." It was unsigned.

Scaevola stared at the note, considering the implications. He reached into the desk's centre drawer and extracted a glass phial, inside which floated a single, unblemished feather. He twirled it between his fingers. "Summon Domitia," he said.

The Junior Clerk's face registered surprise, then terror, then the professional blankness of a man hoping to survive the week.

Domitia arrived before she was sent for. She materialised in the threshold with the ease of someone who had never been denied an entrance, her attire an insult to the prevailing climate and her smile the very picture of plausible deniability. She carried a basket, ostensibly for collecting reports, but which today was occupied by a padded envelope and, on closer inspection, several wax-sealed packages.

"Tribune," she said, voice airy. "I hope I'm not interrupting. I have several updates from the lower city, and—oh, is that for me?" She pointed to the feather, her eyes agleam.

Scaevola did not rise. "Sit," he said, indicating the opposite chair, which teetered with the memory of the last person to sit in it.

She sat, arranging herself with the precision of a well-aimed insult. "There's a rumour," she said, "that someone is impersonating augurs. I heard it from three different men, two of whom claimed to be the original source." She set the basket on the desk, the envelope on top. "This is for you. Contents verified by the Prefect's own seal."

He opened the envelope, removed its contents—a single, slender blade wrapped in felt. The blade was theatrical, the kind used in comic performances: the tip retracted into the hilt with a mechanical click, exposing a strip of painted red along the edge. Scaevola pressed it against his palm, and it emitted a squeak so dismal it might have been a mouse murdered in its sleep.

Domitia regarded the performance with a faint smirk. "The entire shipment was switched. Someone is planning to make a point, either with farce or with actual knives. Odds are even."

He set the prop blade on the table, studied it as one might a rabid animal in a very small cage. "How many people know of this?"

"Everyone who matters, and most of the city by noon," she said. "The augurs are in a frenzy. There's talk of cancelling the parade, but the city council prefers to 'wait and see'."

Scaevola reached for his log, a scroll devoted to the tracking of civic malfeasance, and added a fresh entry: "Daggers replaced with novelty items. Possible theatrical sabotage. Suspects: Domitia, Licinia, anyone who thinks wine is a conduit for divine messaging." He underlined the last name, then dotted the "i" with unusual violence.

Domitia watched with evident delight. "You know," she said, "you really should consider attending the parade. If it does go off, it promises to be historic. And if it doesn't—well, you'll have the satisfaction of being proven right."

He ignored the jibe. "Your own involvement?"

"I prefer my knives blunt," she said, smile sharpening. "But if you need someone to blame, I'm always available for civic service."

He wrote this down, then filed her under "Recidivists, Capable." "Thank you," he said. "You may go."

She lingered a moment, gaze flickering to the fake dagger, then to the stack of reports crowding his desk. "Take care, Tribune," she said, tone sweet enough to rot a molar. "You never know who might be watching the watchmen."

She departed, leaving behind the faint scent of lemon and conspiracy.

He set the blade aside, fingers drumming a tattoo on the desk. The Junior Clerk, now loitering in the hall, poked his head back through the door. "There's more, sir. The permit requests for the Ides have... multiplied."

Scaevola's eyes narrowed. "Multiplied how?"

"By two and a half, sir. More if you count the unregistered vendors."

Scaevola pulled the stack closer, leafing through the top layer. He found, in quick succession: three requests for additional animal sacrifice quotas ("urgent need for goats, see attached rationale"), a proposal to stage "Rome's largest ever mass augury," and an application from the Theatre of Virtue to deploy "fog machines, dramatic" in all public spaces adjacent to the parade route. There were six new florist licenses, four new street crier permits, and one chillingly vague request for "eighty pounds of red pigment, unscented."

He looked up. The Junior Clerk had begun to fidget, his face pale.

"Fetch me all requests mentioning knives, blades, or the Ides. Sort them by time of receipt."

The Junior Clerk bobbed and disappeared. The door, left ajar, creaked softly in the passing draught. Scaevola closed his eyes, then opened them to stare at the ceiling, which responded with a drop of water that landed squarely on Lady Justice's upturned nose.

He returned to the desk, arranged the props and complaints in two neat columns, and began cross-referencing. The effect was immediate: a web of patterns, each strand of coincidence tying the farce to the real, each real thing undermined by its own absurd shadow. The more he wrote, the more the lines blurred. By the time the Junior Clerk returned—arms trembling beneath another mountain of forms—the distinction was lost.

Scaevola watched as the Clerk attempted to set down the stack, misjudged the weight, and upended an inkwell over the entire surface of the desk. Black fluid spread in a slow-motion disaster, seeping into the scrolls, curling around the prop dagger, staining the stamp apparatus. The Clerk, paralysed by horror, gaped as the darkness advanced.

Scaevola did not move. He regarded the spreading stain with the serenity of a man who had always known, in his bones, that the city would one day drown in its own paperwork. He waited until the ink reached the edge of the desk and dripped, one bead at a time, onto the stone floor below.

The Lady Justice bust watched, her blindfold now fully askew, as if to better appreciate the spectacle.

Scaevola drew a fresh sheet, dipped his quill into the puddle, and wrote:

Conspiracy, or parade—functionally identical. Initiate emergency protocol. Observe and document. The city will not be outwitted by its own joke.

He signed the sheet, stamped it with the one working seal, and set it atop the ruined heap.

Then he sat back, hands folded, and waited for the city's next move. The inkwell, now empty, glistened in the light—a perfect black mirror, reflecting the future and its inevitable stains.

The Tribunal's emergency protocol began, as all things did in Rome, with a form: Form IX-C, "Immediate Personal Reconnaissance—Active Malice Suspected." Within the hour of issuing it, Tribune Scaevola was descending the outer stair of the Tribunal, shoes slicked with rain and determination. He had left his own office in the charge of the Junior Clerk, whose only orders were to "record everything, but nothing twice," a command the boy had taken with the anxious seriousness of a child instructed to guard a sleeping snake.

The Forum's lower arcades were already awake with the hum of unofficial business. Beneath the steps, where the city's legitimate trade surrendered to the more entrepreneurial, vendors had laid out impromptu stalls, each a small dictatorship of pricing and volume. Scaevola moved among them with the posture of a man searching for evidence but expecting only disappointment. Overhead, the sky flexed between drizzle and downpour, punctuated by wind that drove the scents of wet parchment, cheap incense, and the animal exhalations of the next parade's main attractions.

He passed three stalls in succession: the first offering "Authentic Augury Results—Freshly Copied!" with a discount for bulk purchases; the second, a bookbinder peddling "Official Edict Retractions—Pre-Approved by the Senate!"; and the third, a tangle of adolescent scribes hawking "Personal Prophecies, Custom Tailored." At this last, a woman in a blue sash argued with the vendor over whether her predicted misfortune was sufficiently specific. The vendor, a youth not old enough to shave but already scarred from the trade, insisted that doom in general was a safer investment than any single disaster.

Scaevola paused. The rain had intensified, flattening the dust and giving the market the look of a regatta for desperate ideas. He noticed a hooded figure at the next stall, hands buried in the folds of his cloak, posture rigid with guilt. The man was haggling in low tones with a scroll vendor, who, judging by the amount of ink on his person, took his work home nightly.

As Scaevola approached, he caught the tail end of the pitch: "This one's special—fresh off the scriptoria! Says Caesar is not just blessed by the gods, but is the reincarnation of Romulus himself. Limited edition. Only three left, and that's the truth."

The hooded figure drew back, voice pitched just above a whisper. "I'm only interested in the original. Not these—these rewrites."

The vendor grinned, exposing a wedge of teeth that had been rearranged by long commerce in close quarters. "The original? That'll cost you. There's only one, and last I heard, it was on its way to the Temple of Concord for safekeeping. Or burning. Either way, not available for retail."

Scaevola stepped in, voice level and precise. "Is there a problem here?"

The vendor recoiled, then adjusted his pitch. "Not at all, Tribune! Just making a sale to a discerning gentleman. Always happy to provide the city's officials with complimentary samples, should you desire." He gestured with a sweep of the hand that nearly knocked over his stack of "Ides of March Survival Kits."

Scaevola ignored the offer, fixing his attention on the hooded man, who now seemed intent on tunnelling through the ground with sheer force of embarrassment. "Remove the hood," Scaevola said, "and perhaps we can avoid a misunderstanding."

The man complied. It was Decimus Flaccus, and the look on his face was that of a scribe who had just discovered a misspelled god in the middle of a holy incantation.

"Tribune," Decimus said, voice attempting dignity but falling somewhere between apology and plea. "I was only—"

"—gathering evidence," Scaevola finished for him. "For the archives, no doubt."

Decimus managed a nod, clutching a battered scroll to his chest. "It's important to document these events from all perspectives. The city's memory is only as reliable as its witnesses."

The vendor, sensing either an opportunity or an audience, piped up. "I can vouch for him! Just a customer, same as any. No trouble at all." He began sorting through his inventory, holding up another scroll. "This one's a classic—'Beware the Cheekbones of Destiny.' Very popular. I'd give you a discount, but I see you're already well-informed."

Scaevola resisted the urge to throttle the man with his own wares. Instead, he addressed Decimus directly. "If you're here in an official capacity, you should know the Tribunal has initiated a full audit of all prophecies in circulation. Any document deemed seditious will be destroyed, and its originator fined or worse."

Decimus swallowed. "I assure you, Tribune, I am not the originator of anything. I'm merely... concerned about the proliferation."

"Proliferation?" Scaevola said. "It's an epidemic. I've seen less viral behaviour in a public latrine."

The vendor, undeterred, produced a fresh roll and unspooled it for their inspection. "Perhaps the Tribune would prefer a prophecy of success? Guaranteed to flatter—money-back if unsatisfied!"

Scaevola glared, and the man shrank, the scroll drooping in defeat.

Before the moment could settle into a rhythm of accusation and denial, a new presence drifted into the scene. Barefoot, her feet blackened by rain and dust, Licinia the ex-augur floated to the edge of the stall, arms draped in what appeared to be several repurposed ceremonial cloths, all of them damp and none matching. She paused beside Scaevola, regarded the trio with a mixture of pity and amusement, and said, "Are we bargaining for the future today, or only for its narrative?"

No one answered. Even the vendor seemed struck dumb by the apparition of a woman who looked half-drowned, half-divine, and entirely at home in the muck of the submarket.

Licinia smiled, the kind of smile that made the rain seem intentional. "If you want the true version," she said, "it's cheaper at the source." She nodded to the vendor, who, recognising a kindred spirit, offered her the scroll gratis. She accepted, broke the seal, and read aloud:

"On the next Ides, a voice will be raised,

Not by augur or scribe but by accident,

And the city will learn, too late,

That destiny is best left to the donkeys."

She handed the scroll to Decimus, who took it with the dazed gratitude of a man reprieved from execution.

Scaevola exhaled, then, realising his lungs had been holding more than just air. "Licinia," he said, "are you involved in this?"

She inclined her head. "Involved is a strong word. I'm conducting market research. The city is undergoing a spiritual audit, and I am merely cataloguing the responses."

The vendor, emboldened by her acceptance, began to hawk his wares again: "Buy now, before the prophecy becomes history!"

Scaevola addressed Licinia in a low voice. "There are too many moving parts. Someone is coordinating the chaos."

Licinia tilted her head. "You flatter the city, Tribune. Chaos is Rome's only native tongue."

She turned to Decimus, who was trying to read the scroll without smearing the ink. "You're a fast learner, Flaccus. The city needs more like you—quick to adapt, slow to betray." She handed him another roll, this one damp from the rain and the wine that had presumably sealed it.

Decimus looked from the scroll to Scaevola. "Should I...?"

Scaevola waved a hand, the motion equal parts dismissal and surrender. "Read it."

Decimus unrolled the parchment. The ink had run, but the message was legible:

Those who chase the truth will be tripped by the lie.

Those who fear the future will find it waiting,

Like a goat at a banquet—unexpected, hungry, and impossible to remove.

A brief silence, filled only by the persistent drizzle and the low mutter of market commerce.

Licinia broke the tension. "There's a story I could tell you, Tribune, about a man who tried to regulate prophecy. It ends badly, but at least no goats were harmed."

Scaevola massaged the bridge of his nose. "If I could ban the future by decree, I would. But until then, I'll settle for containment."

He turned to Decimus. "Go home. Take your archive with you. If you find anything that doesn't rhyme, report

FOURTEEN

The laundry's entrance lay directly beneath the Forum's north colonnade, an architectural oversight never remedied because to fix it would have required noticing it in the first place. The note, left in the hollow of a wine bottle and delivered by a boy with eyes too sharp for his own good, directed Decimus Flaccus there at dusk. It was written in a cipher familiar to all who had once sat the second level grammar exams: every third letter, then the remainder in reverse. It spelled, with minimal ambiguity, "DO NOT BE LATE. / BRING NOTHING. / KNOCK, THEN WAIT."

Decimus complied, though he brought his satchel. He was incapable of not bringing his satchel. He arrived precisely seven minutes late, hoping this would register as both prompt and fashionably wary. The stairwell reeked of old tallow and boiled vinegar, and descended in a spiral just tight enough to hint at the prospect of never quite emerging again.

He reached the bottom, blinked away the sting, and was greeted by the sight of what might have passed for a minor bathhouse, had the clientele not consisted entirely of togas. Bronze vats lined the walls, each seething with a froth of ash, chalk, and water so hot the air above shimmered in agony. A system of ropes and pulleys had been devised to hoist sodden garments from one vat to another, creating a slow, pendulous ballet of dripping linen and steam. Above, hundreds of togas in various shades of off-white hung like the souls of dead senators waiting final judgement.

In the centre of it all, enthroned on a stool varnished by generations of spilled lye, sat Domitia. She wore her usual uniform—homespun shift, sleeves rolled, feet bare—and a string of blue glass beads that flashed with every motion of her neck. Around her, three women and two boys, folding, sorting, and occasionally holding up undergarments to the light with the scepticism of professional examiners.

"Welcome to the Vestal Rinse," she said, without looking up from the tunic she was darning. "If you're here to lodge a complaint, take a number and try again in the next life."

Decimus cleared his throat, to little effect. The steam had rendered his voice sodden. "I was summoned."

Domitia looked up, one eyebrow raised to an altitude not found on most faces. "You were invited. Summons are for people we expect to obey." She flicked a glance at the satchel. "Leave it by the door. You won't need it unless you're planning to do your own laundry."

He hesitated, then obeyed. The satchel, as always, landed with a squelch.

She gestured to a battered bench opposite her throne. "Sit. Mind the bucket. That's where we keep the secrets."

He sat, careful to avoid the bucket, which overflowed with something grey and possibly alive.

Domitia resumed her sewing. "I trust you enjoyed the spectacle at the Forum this morning. It's not every day a donkey achieves such instant celebrity."

Decimus fought to maintain composure. "You heard?"

"Half the city heard. The other half pretended not to, which is why it'll be twice as loud tomorrow." She set aside the tunic, reached for a cup of something steaming and brown, and sipped. "Tea?" she offered. "Or do you prefer the native poisons of the scriptoria?"

He declined with a gesture. "I've come for answers, not comfort."

"Then you're in the wrong place," said Domitia. "Laundry is about comfort. Also, erasure. Which I suspect is why you're here." She inspected the next tunic, discovered a rip, and commenced to patch it with the speed of someone who measured time in stains per hour.

Decimus tried a more direct approach. "You were seen at the Forum. Afterwards, the rumour was everywhere. That's not an accident."

"Nothing is," Domitia replied. "You of all people should know that." She eyed him over the rim of her cup. "But if you're asking whether I started the prophecy, the answer is: no. If you're asking whether I helped spread it, the answer is: does it matter?"

He waited, the silence filled only by the distant gurgle of overworked drains and the ceaseless snap of wet linen.

She set her cup aside. "You look terrible, Flaccus. Has anyone told you that lately?"

"Only my mother," he said, surprised.

"She lied. You looked worse then."

He gave her a thin smile. "You invited me to discuss the prophecy."

She leaned back, hands folded in her lap. "You're asking questions no one wants answered." She tipped her chin toward the nearest cauldron, from which a cloud of scalded citrus peel emerged. "You know how this works, don't you? Someone invents a lie. The lie is repeated. Eventually, the lie becomes more useful than the truth. Then someone tries to 'fix' it. Which is where the trouble begins."

He nodded, but said, "This wasn't supposed to be a lie. It was meant as a—"

"Parody?" Domitia supplied. "Satire? Public warning, cleverly disguised as nonsense?" She retrieved a needle from between her teeth. "Let me save you the effort. Rome does not do irony. If the city laughs, it's because it expects blood."

The women in the corner, folding a mountain of children's tunics, tittered at something said just below audible range. Domitia ignored them.

Decimus felt the sweat bead at his temples, unsure whether it was from the heat or the pace of the exchange. "There's more," he said. "A missing scroll, copied from the original. Hortensius claims it was lost in the archives."

Domitia snorted. "He also claims his debts are a form of personal investment. That's not a man who misplaces anything."

"He seemed... frightened."

Domitia's smile faded. "Good. Means he's still smarter than the average senator." She stood, stretched, and gestured for him to follow her. "Come. You should see this."

He followed, past the boiling vats and the gauntlet of judging women, to a small back chamber. Here, the steam was less a cloud and more a soup. On the wall, dozens of laundry baskets were stacked to the ceiling, each labelled in red wax: "To Be Repaired", "For Discreet Disposal", "Possibly Salvageable", and one, at the very top, "To Be Bleached – Prophetic."

Domitia pulled this last basket down, revealing a scroll, soaked and puckered, tied with string. "Found it this morning. Came in with the rest of the week's soiled sheets. Would've missed it, if not for the fact that most prophecy doesn't get laundered."

Decimus reached for it, hands trembling.

"Careful," Domitia said, not unkindly. "If there's anything left to read, it'll be warped by now."

He unrolled it, fingers aching with anticipation. Most of the ink had bled into a confused haze, but here and there a line survived, wavering like the memory of a rumour. He read aloud:

"When laurel lies low and cheekbones rise,
The tide shall shift with Empire's guise,
A voice once small will echo loud,
And truth will drown in a marching crowd—"

He stopped. The next lines had merged into a single puddle, as if the parchment itself had wept for what it must contain.

Domitia watched his face. "Dramatic," she said. "Not the usual menu of curses. You think it's real?"

He looked up. "It's the handwriting. I know it. It's mine." He paused. "But I don't remember writing this."

She took the scroll from him, handled it as one might a sickly animal. "If you want it back, it's yours. But I'd recommend keeping it here. In case someone comes asking."

"Who would ask you?" he said, then regretted it.

"Everyone comes to the laundry," Domitia said. "Eventually." She tucked the scroll into a compartment behind the baskets. "You're not the only one with enemies, Flaccus. But your enemies are better at remembering what you owe them."

He said, "Why are you helping me?"

She regarded him, then shrugged. "My interests are practical. You're a good customer. If you die, I get to keep your desk."

The steam, for a moment, seemed to settle. Decimus felt the weight of every word, the way a city feels the weight of its own future.

She turned to go, then paused. "There's someone looking for you. Not the Tribune. Not the augurs. Higher."

"Who?" he said.

She grinned, all teeth and calculation. "If I told you, you'd never sleep again. And if you don't sleep, I lose a customer. So, for now, keep to your own end of the city.

And if you must write, write nothing you wouldn't want performed in public by a donkey."

He nodded, uncertain whether this was a threat, a warning, or an offer of partnership.

"Thank you," he said, and meant it.

Domitia returned to the main room, where the women and boys had conspired to hang a fresh batch of togas along the ceiling. She called out, "Make sure the senator's linen gets double-starched. If he stains it again, we'll have to boil him in it."

A ripple of laughter, soft but merciless.

Decimus retrieved his satchel and let himself out, the air on the stairwell cold by comparison, the street above so bright and sharp it felt like punishment.

He walked, scroll still damp in his mind, the words etching themselves with every step. At the edge of the Forum, he paused, looked back, and saw the steam still rising, the togas flapping in the half-light like ghosts.

He turned away, resolved to make his own edits before someone else wrote his ending.

Tribune Scaevola arrived at the Temple of Janus with his shoes freshly cleaned and his expectations otherwise unchanged. The temple, recently downgraded from "Centre of Civic Harmony" to "Heritage Site (Unfunded)," had survived its last fire only by virtue of being mostly stone and, in places, already reduced to cinder.

Scaevola ascended the steps, pausing only to brush ash from the lintel, and rapped at the iron-banded door.

It was opened, after an interval long enough to suggest careful rehearsal, by an acolyte. The boy wore the hollow-eyed expression of one recently introduced to either religion or overtime.

"Tribune," he said, blinking with the effort. "You're early."

"I'm never early," said Scaevola. "Everyone else is late." He handed the boy two folders, each marked "URGENT – Not That Anyone Cares," and followed him down a hall lined with busts of Janus, every face chipped or bisected.

They passed through the nave, where what remained of the congregation—three pensioned augurs and a musician on retainer—were engaged in a slow-motion quarrel over the proper orientation of a statue. At the back, a door led to the archives, which had once housed sacred calendars and now served as overflow storage for the city's more ambitious hardware.

The annex was a windowless chamber lit by two narrow slits and a guttering lamp. The walls were lined with racks, each bearing an arsenal of ceremonial weapons, ritual implements, and, for reasons lost to precedent, several crates of commemorative spoons.

The custodian of this realm was the priest himself: a man of indeterminate age, draped in saffron robes, hair dyed the colour of ash, his hearing so unreliable he had long since adopted the habit of reading lips.

"Tribune Scaevola," he said, with the air of one

reciting a curse that had never quite worked. "Welcome to the Temple."

The acolyte, still trembling from the stairs, retrieved the URGENT folders and set them on the main table. The priest leaned over them, squinted, and said, "So many daggers. Are these all for the Ides, or are you planning ahead?"

"I'd like to see the crate," said Scaevola.

The priest shrugged, performed a slow three-point turn, and led the way to a section of shelving near the east wall. He tapped a wooden crate with the end of a ceremonial staff, and, with the aid of a crowbar, levered off the lid.

Scaevola looked inside, then looked again. The crate was filled to the brim with knives, each identical, each with a blade that collapsed into the hilt upon contact with the merest resistance. They were the kind used in stage comedies—retractable, spring-loaded, and painted in such a way that even a particularly gullible child would spot the joke.

The priest watched him, face studiously blank.

"Are these the official issue?" Scaevola asked.

"Only the best for the gods," the priest said, deadpan. "If you'd prefer the real thing, you'll have to talk to the City Armoury. We're not allowed so much as a letter opener without written permission."

Scaevola reached in, extracted one of the knives, and pressed the blade to his palm. It disappeared with a cheerful click. He dropped it back into the crate, where it landed with a sound like a bundle of celery.

"These are for the public sacrifice?" he said.

"Modern interpretive trends," the priest replied. "We've had complaints. Last year, someone said the sight of blood made them faint. The year before, the actor missed the goat entirely and slashed a deacon's robe. It's safer this way."

"And the other implements?" Scaevola gestured to a shelf marked "SPECIAL RITUALS – DO NOT REMOVE."

The priest led him to it. Here, in addition to the expected assortment of sickles and hammers, there was a single, plush cudgel, dyed gold, with a loop at one end for easy carrying.

"Festival of Childhood Innocence," the priest explained. "If you can think of a less offensive way to batter iniquity, I'd like to hear it."

Scaevola set his jaw. "Who signs for these deliveries?"

The priest motioned to the acolyte, who produced a battered ledger and opened it to the most recent entries. Scaevola took the book, scanned the list, and found what he sought:

"*RECEIVED: 40 units ceremonial dagger (stage), 12 units symbolic cudgel (plush), 1 unit crisis hotline scroll (sealed). Signed: 'Office of Official Histories, Deputy for Ritual Oversight.'*" The signature was rendered as a looping initial and a slash, the name beneath redacted with an aggressive line of ink.

"Why the redaction?" Scaevola asked.

The acolyte blushed. "It's the custom, sir. For deniability. No one wants their name on the paperwork if it goes wrong."

The priest coughed. "We find it improves accountability, in the sense that no one is accountable. The old ways are the best."

Scaevola closed the ledger. "Do you have the original delivery slip?"

The boy nodded, vanished into a cupboard, and returned with a scroll tied in blue ribbon. Scaevola broke the seal, scanned the contents, and found the same pattern: an order for theatrical daggers, signed off by "Office of Official Histories," this time with a different, equally indecipherable mark.

He turned to the priest. "You understand that this is not a mistake. Someone wanted the parade armed with nothing but toys."

The priest smiled. "A great many people in this city prefer it that way."

Scaevola bristled. "This isn't just theatre. It's fraud. If a real attack were to occur—"

"Then it would be the first real thing to happen in this temple in decades," said the priest. He reached into the crate, selected a knife at random, and twirled it between his fingers with surprising dexterity. "We've all learned to perform our roles, Tribune. Yours is to be outraged, mine is to officiate the sacrifice, and theirs—" he gestured to the acolyte, who promptly dropped a tray of spoons— "is to keep the whole thing afloat."

Scaevola regarded him for a long moment. "Who else knows about the switch?"

The priest considered. "Anyone who cares to look. No one cares to look."

"I do," Scaevola said.

"Then you're a rare bird," the priest replied, "and a soon-to-be-very-lonely one."

Scaevola pocketed the blue-ribboned scroll. "If anyone asks, these are now under audit. No one touches them until I say so."

The priest bowed. "Take them all, if you like. I prefer my knives sharp."

He left, the acolyte scurrying after, arms cradling the folder and ledger. In the nave, the three augurs were still at war with the statue, now attempting to rotate it with a length of curtain rod and a system of pulleys borrowed from the laundry below. Scaevola ignored them, taking the side passage to the street.

Outside, the rain had returned, this time with a commitment. He stood beneath the overhang, opened the folder, and compared the two delivery signatures. The first, he now realised, was a near-perfect match for a memo he had encountered a week prior: the same extravagant flourish, the same artful illegibility.

He extracted the earlier memo from his own satchel, spread it alongside the new one, and studied them as if the ink would confess. Slowly, the sense of it emerged: a pattern, deliberate, and growing.

He replaced the documents, careful to keep them dry. Someone, somewhere, was rewriting not just the speeches but the record of the city itself. The weapons were the least of it; the true danger was in the control of the script.

He squared his shoulders, mentally drafted the next three steps of inquiry, and braced himself to descend into the next layer of Rome's ongoing experiment with truth.

As he moved off, the clouds parted just enough to let a shaft of light strike the temple's entrance. It illuminated, for an instant, the chipped twin faces of Janus—one looking forward, the other back, both equally unimpressed by the prospect of tomorrow.

Scaevola nodded at the gods, as a professional courtesy, then vanished into the wet.

FIFTEEN

Decimus Flaccus stared at the tent and the tent, in turn, stared back. It had been pitched, with due disregard for public order and the unwritten rules of metaphysics, directly in front of the official augury temple's pillared entrance. Its fabric, borrowed from failed festival banners and what he suspected was an old military tarp, shuddered in the late-morning wind, each gust carrying an aroma that mingled incense with the unmistakable tang of livestock. A placard, hand-lettered in a style alternating between desperation and menace, announced: "Today Only—Bacchic Omens & Interpretive Chanting. All Welcome. BYO Offering."

He checked the slip of papyrus again. The instructions had been written by a hand whose only rival for nervousness was his own. "Attend. Be seen. Remain upright." The first and third seemed attainable, provided he did not attempt the second with too much enthusiasm. He flexed his fingers, trying to work the morning's ink cramps from his knuckles, and ducked inside.

The air, if such it could be called, was a cloud of burning juniper, spilt resin, and the sort of cheese once used as a biological weapon during the Etruscan incursions. His eyes watered instantly. The tent was smaller than it looked, its space dominated by a patchwork carpet, five cushions, three incense burners, a table bearing half a dozen jars of suspicious fluid, and, occupying the centre like an inconvenient boulder, a goat of exceptional size and misgiving. Its horns described a parabola that would have pleased the finest mathematicians, had any survived the previous night's wine.

Licinia, ex-augur and current engine of ceremonial disaster, stood barefoot on a wooden crate at the tent's far end. She wore a robe dyed the precise shade of fermenting grape, and her hair, woven with laurel and the odd feather, radiated in all directions as if struck by lightning or committee. In her left hand, she brandished a cup; in her right, a sprig of fennel, which she used alternately as pointer, conductor's baton, and disciplinary rod for the goat.

"Decimus!" she called, spotting him with the predator's gaze common to theatre directors and the acutely unemployed. "I trust you bring a suitable offering. And a witness, if possible?"

He glanced behind him. No one had followed. "I come alone," he said, voice muffled by the smoke and immediate regret.

"Then you must play both roles. Enter." She raised the cup, and the ritual began.

The first stage was simple enough: a series of invocations to Bacchus, delivered in a hybrid of High Latin, kitchen Greek, and what sounded suspiciously like the local butcher's patois. Each phrase required the pouring of wine in spirals on the ground, which the goat regarded with wounded professionalism. At the third spiral, Licinia set the cup down and recited, "Let those who seek the future learn first to endure the present." She stared directly at Decimus, then drank.

The second stage was "interpretive." She circled the tent, arms raised, intoning the sacred words as she picked her way through the cushions and the increasingly nervous goat. She drew a chalk line on Decimus's brow, a circle on the carpet, and an S-shaped mark on the tent pole. "These are the boundaries of prophecy," she explained. "Also, the locations of prior accidents."

The third stage required a demonstration of "divinatory receptivity," which, in Licinia's model, meant taking a seat and contemplating the goat's entrails. Not by sacrifice—the beast had survived too many such ceremonies to participate voluntarily—but by close study of its digestive habits.

Licinia produced a battered scroll from the folds of her sleeve, consulted it, and pronounced, "The omens are favourable, if somewhat sluggish." She flicked the fennel at Decimus. "Place your hands upon the goat."

He hesitated. "Is it safe?"

She ignored him, and the goat, with the resignation of the long-employed, shuffled closer and deposited its full weight onto his shins. He nearly toppled.

"Now," said Licinia, voice dropping to a register somewhere between conspiratorial and funereal, "repeat after me: 'Spill not the wine of knowledge. Cast not the cheese of wisdom before the unready.'"

Decimus complied, and the ritual, if anything, intensified. Licinia spun three times, then stopped, swaying gently. The goat chewed its cud and glared at him with a wisdom unblunted by the recent ordeal.

It was at this point that the tent flap parted, admitting three more participants: a pair of acolytes in patched robes and a woman with the bearing of a professional mourner and the dress sense to match. They arranged themselves at the perimeter, eyes never leaving Licinia.

She nodded at the new arrivals, then drained the remainder of the cup. "Now comes the reading of the future," she said. "Decimus, you are the vessel. The city, the storm. Let us see if the omens choose to speak."

He braced himself. Licinia seized the jar labelled "Prophetic Catalyst" and poured a generous measure over the goat's back, then onto the carpet. The smell, already bad, achieved a new plateau.

She pressed both hands to Decimus's temples. "Do you see it?" she hissed.

He saw nothing but stars and possibly the ancestors of most present-day cheeses. "Yes," he managed.

"Describe."

He struggled. "A city... drowning in ink. A donkey at the head of a parade. Citizens chanting... something about cheekbones. The augurs... asleep at their posts."

Licinia's eyes widened. "This is good. This is very good." She turned to the acolytes. "Record it. All of it."

One acolyte fumbled for a writing tablet; the other,

slower, missed the cue and instead reached for a jar of olives, which he ate with the grim determination of a man hoping to avoid being volunteered for demonstration.

Licinia raised her arms again. "Let Bacchus be praised, for the omens have spoken! Rome's fate is upon us. Let the prophecy be known: When cheekbones rise, and augurs slumber, and the donkey is crowned, the city will be—" She paused, vision flickering. "—liberated. Or possibly mildly inconvenienced."

She swayed, then, with a suddenness that defied physics, fell backwards off the crate. The acolytes rushed to her aid, but she waved them off, rolled to her feet, and launched into the ceremonial dance, which involved little more than a shuffle and a great deal of arm-flailing. The goat, perhaps sensing a rival for attention, bleated so loud the tent nearly collapsed.

It was at this moment that the fire started.

No one was quite sure how it happened, but the consensus later was that a loose sleeve, a wayward elbow, and a neglected candle had conspired against the drapery. In an instant, the rear wall of the tent was a sheet of orange.

Decimus sprang to his feet, upending the goat. "The tent—"

Licinia, hair now ablaze at the tips, seized the jar of wine and doused her own head. "It's tradition," she announced, voice distorted by smoke.

The acolytes panicked. One attempted to beat out the flames with a sheaf of prophecies, which only served to set those alight; the other staggered in circles, shrieking that the omens were now doubly unfavourable. The mourner wept with professional conviction, and the goat, after a brief but spirited attempt at escape, fainted.

Decimus tried to recall the fire drill from his days in the archives, but the only instruction he remembered was "rescue the documents, then the staff." There were no documents, and the staff were in varying stages of combustion.

He grabbed the nearest bucket, dumped its contents (pickled onions, by the smell), and filled it with wine from the largest jar. He flung the mixture onto the burning wall, quenching most of the flames but also dissolving a substantial portion of the tent.

In the aftermath, the inside of the tent was a swamp of wine, melted wax, and the smouldering remains of Bacchic paraphernalia. Licinia, hair extinguished but now tinted violet, emerged from the wreckage carrying the goat in her arms like a martyr. She deposited it on the nearest cushion, then turned to Decimus.

"You," she said, with the gravity of a woman who had seen through the veil, "are destined for great and terrible things."

He stared at his hands, now stained purple and sticky. "I'd rather just edit the records," he said.

She laughed, and the acolytes joined in, their hysteria barely masking the horror. The mourner, now out of a job, drifted away into the smoke. The goat, miraculously recovered, licked wine from the carpet and regarded Decimus with something like approval.

Licinia limped to the tent flap, held it open, and

bowed him through. "Go," she said. "Tell the city what you have seen. And take this—" She handed him a scrap of singed scroll. "For the archives."

He took it, and, weaving slightly, made his way back into the world.

The city, for once, was silent. He walked, slow and careful, to the foot of the temple steps, where he sat and unrolled the scroll. The ink had run, but the message was legible:

Beware the man with cheekbones like thunder, for he shall write the fate of Rome and all who dwell therein. Let the parade be joyous, but know that at its end waits the donkey, and the truth it carries will not be denied.

He folded the scroll, tucked it into his satchel, and stared at the sky, which was now streaked with the colour of old bruises and, above the city's haze, the faintest suggestion of something new.

He laughed, once, then twice, and for the first time since he had been recruited, felt the possibility that the city might one day surprise even itself.

He stood, checked his reflection in a puddle—still recognisable, if a little more purple—and set off for home.

The city resumed its noise, and in the morning, the rumour would spread: the omens had been read, the future foretold, and Rome—one way or another—was doomed to continue.

The Office of Official Histories had always been damp, but this evening it was competing with itself for a new record. Decimus Flaccus perched at the edge of his stool, his toga still clinging in cold patches where wine and prophecy had commingled. The fingers of his left hand were purple from clutching the salvaged scroll; his right, ever the optimist, attempted to dry the sopping document by holding it to the office brazier, whose only contribution to the task was a weak sigh of sour smoke.

He glanced at the closed window, the glass furred with mildew and, in one corner, the historic remains of a moderately successful wasp. Outside, the city howled in celebration, or possibly commiseration, at the day's augury. Inside, the only noise was the sizzle of his damp robe and the steady drip from the ceiling onto a growing patch of green in the far corner.

He tried to read the recovered lines. The ink had bled into fantastic shapes, the sort that would later be discovered by philosophers to contain the secrets of geometry and, perhaps, cheese-making. Most of the text was gone, but one phrase repeated, ever fainter:

When glory is paraded, Rome shall slip.

He set it aside, unsure whether to laugh or footnote it for the next poor wretch. The rest of the scroll was an inebriated haze of misplaced metaphors, with brief, bright flashes of pure despair. Even the goat, which appeared three times in as many lines, seemed to have lost the thread by the end.

He propped his chin on his hand, allowing a thin trickle of relief to replace the usual panic. Today's prophecy was not his doing. If anything, he was a victim

—of ambition, of rituals, of goats. If the city burned, at least it would be for reasons that no historian, however inventive, could lay at his doorstep.

The door rattled. He started upright, nearly upsetting the brazier. It was Scribonius, his supervisor and, on bad days, the Office's chief apologist.

"Flaccus!" said Scribonius, all joviality and no content. "You're here late. Very good, very good. Dedication. Rome is built on it, or so the commemorative mugs keep insisting."

Decimus rose, nearly tearing his toga in the process. "Sir. I was just—"

"No need to explain," said Scribonius, waving a hand slicked with lamp oil. "Word travels. I hear the morning's ceremony was... memorable."

He hesitated, then added, with the precision of a man quoting a memo, "The Ministry of Moral Memory has requested an official version by sunrise. Uplifting, dignified, and, if possible, faith-enhancing."

Decimus felt his lips move, but heard nothing come out.

Scribonius loomed closer, his smile now a blueprint for future disappointment. "What you witnessed, Flaccus, was not a failure of ritual. It was an opportunity. The city is hungry for assurance. It needs a version of events that will keep the markets open and the children in school."

"Even if it's a lie?" Decimus asked, instantly regretting the question.

Scribonius beamed. "If it's in the record, it's the truth. You know this. I know this. The goats know this." He paused, as if waiting for a goat to respond. "Simply... shape the narrative. There's no need to mention the animal, or the fire, or the questionable cheese. Focus on the divine serenity. The communal spirit. Rome, standing united at the threshold of tomorrow."

Decimus nodded, in the same way a condemned man nods when handed the noose.

Scribonius clapped his shoulder, leaving a print of something sticky. "Good lad. I've sent for a fresh scroll. Be sure it's delivered to the Ministry by first light." He leaned in, voice lowering. "This is your chance, Flaccus. Don't waste it on footnotes."

He left, door slamming with bureaucratic authority.

Decimus sat, the air thick with mildew, ink, and impending revisionism. He looked at his notes, then at the blank scroll unfurled before him. The lines of the prophecy haunted his mind, but he knew what was expected. Rome did not want the truth. Rome wanted reassurance, wrapped in a ribbon and delivered before the next parade.

He picked up his pen, hands still stained, and began:

On the morning of the Ides, the people of Rome gathered to receive the blessing of Bacchus. The augur Licinia, radiant with devotion, led the city in sacred rites, offering prayers for abundance, unity, and peace. A vision appeared, clear and without ambiguity: The empire would flourish, its citizens bound together by shared purpose and the enduring favour of the gods. There were songs. There was laughter. There was hope.

He paused, considered, then appended:

As the ceremony concluded, the signs were clear to all:

Rome would persist, undaunted, into a new season of prosperity.

He stared at the words. They might have been true, in a sense, if you stood far enough away and squinted until reality blurred.

A tap at the window interrupted his reverie. It was the office pigeon, come to collect the overnight missives. Decimus attached the scroll, sealed it, and watched as the bird flapped off into the drizzle, entirely unburdened by the gravity of its cargo.

He slumped back, the day catching up to him all at once. The wetness of his robe, the staleness of the air, the ache in his spine from a dozen bad chairs and a lifetime of bending to the will of men who would never read what he wrote.

He closed his eyes and, for a moment, imagined a city where the truth mattered more than the illusion. It was an uncomfortable fantasy, best left in the archive of dreams.

When he opened them again, the office was dark. The only light came from the brazier, where the last scrap of the prophecy curled and smoked, its ink rising in thin, accusatory wisps. He watched it burn to ash, then brushed the remains onto the floor.

He wiped his hands, gathered his things, and made for the door. As he stepped into the hall, he thought he heard the echo of laughter—Licinia's, perhaps, or the goat's, or the city's.

The Office of Official Histories would have its narrative. Rome would have its parade. And in the morning, the world would carry on, exactly as before.

But for a moment, at least, the truth had been written.

He left, the sound of his footsteps swallowed by the wet stone and the infinite capacity of Rome to believe what it needed.

SIXTEEN

Domitia presided over a long, battered table, her hands folding linen in a manner that was both punitive and ceremonial. Today, she had appropriated a milk crate as her throne, and from this elevation she had the full measure of the yard and anyone foolish enough to enter it.

The donkey was present, as advertised. It stood tethered to a corner post, chewing on what appeared, from a distance, to be a bundle of leaf. On closer inspection, the leaf resolved into the remains of a scroll, its text effaced by saliva and its lower edge worked to a pulp. The beast fixed him with a gaze both sceptical and familiar, then returned to its appointed task.

Domitia did not look up until Decimus was three steps from the table, at which point she announced, "You're early, but not enough to be a surprise."

He replied, "I thought perhaps you'd appreciate a customer not covered in last night's sauce."

She flicked a look at his toga, which had developed a

fresh patina of city grime, then at the satchel beneath his arm. "Everyone's a customer, eventually. Even if they come empty-handed."

He hesitated, aware that any attempt at formality would be wasted. Instead, he asked, "Do you ever run out of clean linen?"

She answered by folding the current sheet into a square so perfect it threatened to upend geometry, then tossing it onto the growing stack at her side. "Never. There's always another supply. The Senate is addicted to pageantry, the priests to self-abasement, and the rest to the illusion of order. I just provide the costume changes."

He said, "They say you're laundering more than linen."

She smiled, but only with her eyes. "The city launders everything. I just do it more efficiently."

He took the opening. "The prophecy. You're involved."

She made a sound halfway between a snort and a cough. "Is that what they're calling it now? I preferred the earlier version—'a misfiled disaster.' It had a certain transparency."

He glanced at the donkey, which was now working the scroll with the dedication of a scribe assigned to public records. "You know it's spreading. The augurs, the street performers, even the bathhouses—everyone's quoting the same lines. It's almost as if someone wants them to."

"Someone always wants them to," she said. "But rarely do they pay as well as you'd expect."

He took a step closer. "Who's funding it?"

She folded another toga, this one stained in a spiral of red. She held it up, inspected the blemish, then extended it for his inspection. "What colour is that, do you think? Wine, or blood?"

He looked. The stain ran in a loop, as if a careless hand had tried and failed to uncork a bottle in motion. "Depends who was drinking."

She nodded, satisfied, and added it to a separate pile. "The city prefers its mysteries unresolved."

He said, "This isn't just about the prophecy. I heard you've been contracted to supply costumes for the Triumph."

This time, she did look up, the blue of her eyes catching the brief slant of morning sun. "It's a parade, Flaccus. Of course I'm involved. Who else could dress three hundred plebeians in matching tunics and not lose her mind?"

He pressed. "But these are not ordinary costumes. They're duplicates. For every official, a double. For every guard, a mask."

She shrugged. "The Senate wants spectacle. The people want a spectacle they can believe in. My job is to make sure neither group is disappointed."

"And the donkey?"

She grinned. "He's a natural. Been cast as himself in every major festival since the Flood."

He tried to steer the conversation. "The prophecy says the donkey will see everything, but not speak."

"Which makes him the wisest in Rome," she said. "If you're here to interrogate, ask quickly. I have an order to fill by noon, and the next batch of starch is aggressive."

He decided bluntness would get him further than finesse. "Did you help write it?"

She resumed folding. "I help everyone write everything. People bring me secrets on their tunics, bribes in their cuffs. Most are too dull to be worth a second rinse. The prophecy, though—that was something different. It stuck."

He said, "You're deflecting."

"Not at all," she replied, smoothing a crease. "If you want names, you're out of luck. If you want motives, it's always the same: money, fear, the love of a good riot."

He watched her work for a moment, then said, "I heard the costumes for the Triumph are not just for show. There's a rumour of smoke pots, rigged carts, and a second line of marchers."

She did not pause, but her tone sharpened. "Who told you that?"

He hesitated. "Let's call it an accidental leak."

She said, "Nothing leaks by accident, Flaccus. If you know about the smoke pots, you also know that someone intends to use them. And that someone is paying through the nose to keep their hands clean."

He let the silence expand, hoping she would fill it.

She did. "There's a group. Not from the usual quarters. They want the parade to succeed and fail, both at once. They want the people to see glory, then chaos, then nothing at all. And they want the city to remember only the confusion."

He asked, "Why?"

She handed him the stained toga. "Because in confusion, nobody is to blame. It's the safest place in the world."

He said, "Do you know who hired you?"

She shrugged. "It's always a friend of a friend. This time, the friend had a senator's ring and the manners of an executioner. If you want a name, ask at the Temple. If you want to live, don't."

He accepted the toga. It was still damp, and the stain, he realised, was neither wine nor blood, but a careful mixture of both. "And the prophecy?"

She finished the last fold, stacked it on the pile, and turned to the donkey. It had now finished the scroll and was looking at her expectantly.

She untied it, patted its flank, and said, "He sees everything, Flaccus. He just doesn't talk."

He looked at the donkey, then at her. "If I come back tomorrow, will you give me another answer?"

She shook her head. "Tomorrow the city will have a new question. That's how it survives."

He nodded, realising the interview was over.

As he stepped from the yard, the donkey brayed once —short, sharp, and not entirely unlike laughter.

He turned at the end of the alley. Domitia was already at work again, folding, sorting, preparing the next round of disguises for a city that never wanted to be seen for what it was.

He walked away, the sound of linen snapping in the wind following him down the street, and wondered whether anyone would recognise the city when the parade was over.

SEVENTEEN

The city's faith in the miraculous powers of civic logistics was, to Decimus's mind, its only true religion. Every disaster that befell the Republic—famine, invasion, the annual collapse of public morals—was met first with a sacrifice, then a parade, and finally a committee. Today, as he ducked into the Triumph Supply Depot, he realised that Rome's entire future currently rested on a warehouse staffed by people who had never, to his knowledge, successfully completed a single form.

The depot, located in a decommissioned grain barn near the Circus Maximus, exuded the peculiar odour of optimism gone mouldy. Bundles of silk bunting draped from the rafters, each labelled "Triumphal (Large, Redundant)" in two or more languages. Along the eastern wall, a rack of papier-mâché elephants awaited paint or decommission, depending on the state of the city's finances. Everywhere, the fine grit of gold leaf and sawdust drifted, settling on crates marked "TRI-UMPHAL CONFETTI – DO NOT INGEST" and several battered amphorae which had once contained either wine or sacrificial oil and now hosted only the promise of disappointment.

At the centre of the confusion stood Aulus Malleolus, the city's least voluntary master of ceremonies. He wore his toga slung low on the hip, exposing a chest best described as ambitious, and paced a groove into the stone floor while consulting a clipboard, a wax tablet, and his own mounting sense of catastrophe. He turned, mid-pace, and fixed Decimus with the stare of a man who would pay any price, up to and including homicide, for one functioning assistant.

"Flaccus! Thank the gods, or whoever's left. We have a situation." He thrust the clipboard forward, nearly impaling Decimus in the sternum. "Do you see this?"

Decimus did, and immediately wished he had not. The top sheet bore a neat rendering of the parade schedule: 9:00, Sacrifice of the Noble Ox. 9:30, Pre-procession Benediction. 10:00, Assembly at the Arch of Triumph. The entire column for "Laurel Crown Ceremony" had been X'd out, with a note in the margin: "Pending re-delivery from offsite. See attached."

He said, "I take it the laurels have not arrived?"

Aulus barked a mirthless laugh. "The laurels have not only failed to arrive, but they have also vanished from the manifest. I have men combing the Aventine and the entire staff of Civic Flora locked in a closet until they produce answers or a confession."

Decimus set his satchel on a crate marked "Processional Accoutrements – Emergency Use Only" and tried to bring order to the mess. "Was there a backup shipment? Or an alternative—"

"Don't you think I thought of that?" snapped Aulus, who was now several pages ahead in the spiral of his own undoing. "We can't use pine. The augurs say it sends the wrong message. Olive is reserved for peace treaties, which, as you may have noticed, is not in fashion." He gestured toward the far end of the barn, where a row of hollowed helmets awaited laurel crowns with the mournful patience of condemned men.

A junior scribe, hauling a crate nearly his own size, nearly collided with Decimus, then sidled past with the apologetic gait of a man who had seen too much and retained nothing. Overhead, a cloud of dust descended from the mezzanine, where two workers were arguing in stage whispers over whether the Triumph's lead float should feature the likeness of Caesar, a composite hero, or, in a cost-saving measure, the city's last successful lottery winner.

In the midst of this, Gaius the Landlord emerged from behind a curtain of red bunting, cheeks pink with either exertion or a surfeit of optimism. He carried a mug of something foaming, and wore the look of a man determined to enjoy every minute not spent at his actual job.

He greeted Decimus with a conspiratorial wink, then addressed Aulus: "If the laurels have gone walkabout, why not just make more? There's a whole park of the stuff behind the Subura. Worst case, you have to bribe a gardener."

Aulus rounded on him. "It must be from the Sacred Grove, Gaius. The augurs certified the shipment, sealed it with—" he riffled the clipboard, found a document, and waved it like a battle flag, "—this wax. If we substitute, the omens are invalid, and I'm the one who gets sacrificed."

"Leaves are leaves, aren't they?" said Gaius, who had never once been hindered by a technicality.

"Not to the union," replied the nearest worker, who had stopped pretending to unload the amphorae. "We're not risking a smiting. Not after what happened at the Bread Festival."

Decimus, who was quietly making notes, interjected: "What did happen at the Bread Festival?"

The worker, emboldened by attention, launched into his story. "Last year, they tried to run the festival with counterfeit wheat. Imported from Carthage. The head baker got a nosebleed and collapsed in the opening ceremony. The omens were so bad they had to burn the entire harvest. No one ate bread for a week."

Aulus rolled his eyes, but made a note anyway. "Fine," he said. "No substitutions. We do it by the book or not at all."

Gaius shrugged, finished his mug, and looked about for a refill.

Decimus examined the logbook, tracing the supply chain from Grove to Depot. A pencilled annotation in the margin caught his eye: "Wreaths redirected per Poetic Mandate 44-XII." He turned the book toward Aulus, who squinted at it with growing alarm.

"Do you have any idea what this means?" Aulus asked, as if Decimus might spontaneously develop a hobby in obscure regulations.

"It looks like someone cited a special order," Decimus said. "A poetic mandate, whatever that is."

Gaius perked up. "Oh, that's mine. I submitted it yesterday. The laurels were meant for the city's poets' society. We're staging a dramatic reading during the Triumph, and I thought—well, no one ever notices the details unless you make a show of it."

Aulus's face achieved a new shade of puce. "You rerouted the sacred laurels for a poetry reading?"

Gaius nodded, unfazed. "It's all part of the spectacle. Besides, I wrote a new ode for the occasion—'In Praise of the Ever-Triumphant'—and it calls for the crowning of a new hero."

"Who," Aulus said, "is presumably you."

Gaius grinned. "If the laurel fits."

Decimus pinched the bridge of his nose. "Where did the delivery go, exactly?"

Gaius consulted the back of his hand, where several addresses had been inscribed in ink. "Temple of Prophetic Recalibration, up on the Aventine. They said they'd keep it safe until the morning."

Aulus staggered back, then collapsed onto the nearest crate. "The last time we trusted the Prophetic Recalibration people, we had to cancel the entire Saturnalia. The omens were 'too ambiguous to proceed'."

A runner, breathless and sticky with what might have been sweat or early-stage panic, burst into the warehouse. "There's a man outside, says he's from the augurs' union. He's demanding to see the parade master. He has a badge."

Aulus clapped his hands together, once, as if to expel a curse. "This is it. This is the end."

Decimus, sensing the approach of a full-blown breakdown, stepped forward. "I'll go. I know some of the priests up there. Maybe I can smooth things over."

Aulus, too far gone for pride, nodded. "Take Gaius. If they won't hand it over, at least you can write them a flattering letter."

Gaius looked delighted. "Road trip!" he said, then grabbed a handful of parade biscuits from a tray and stuffed them into his cloak.

The two of them set off, leaving behind the sound of Aulus dictating a last will and testament to the nearest scribe.

The runner, now out of errands, regarded the two men with something like awe. "Good luck, sirs. The gods are watching."

Gaius beamed. "Let's give them a show, then."

They made their way out, through a corridor of half-built floats and the faint, hopeful sound of a lyre being tuned off-key. Behind them, the city rehearsed its Triumph, blissfully unaware that the difference between glory and total collapse was, as always, measured in leaves.

The Aventine always made Decimus nervous. Even before the Temple's fall from civic grace, he had considered the entire hill a repository for everything the rest of the city preferred to forget. Out-of-date cults, fading noble families, a tendency for mudslides and, at the summit, the Temple of Prophetic Recalibration—a name that, he was certain, had originated as a joke and then simply stuck.

He and Gaius made their way uphill along a path alternately paved in moss and bureaucratic resentment. Gaius provided colour commentary for every landmark —"that's where they exiled the last augur who questioned an omen," "here's the infamous cheese market, closed for public safety, reopened for private consumption"—while Decimus rehearsed diplomatic approaches for dealing with the Temple's priesthood, none of which ended with him being sacrificed to Omen, the sacred goose.

They reached the portico to find the Temple in a state of curated ruin. Its columns had been patched in places with what appeared to be driftwood, and a sign at the entrance—"Pardon our Restoration; Your Fate May Be Delayed"—had, in smaller print, "No Public Urination" appended below.

At the threshold, a custodian in a robe stained with more wine than piety barred their way. "What business?" he intoned, not so much a question as a warning.

Decimus mustered his most official voice. "Laurel delivery. Office of Official Histories. Requisitioned in error, but now urgently required."

The custodian eyed them, weighed the odds of violence, then jerked a thumb toward the nave. "Speak to the Scribe. If the laurels are truly yours, he'll need three witnesses and an oath. Preferably not under the influence."

Gaius attempted to look sober, and failed even to achieve the illusion.

Inside, the nave was a symphony in peeling plaster and the smell of very old incense. The only illumination came from three lamps: one suspended over the altar, one above the Scribe's desk, and one apparently wired to a tripwire near the confessional. At the altar's base, a large white goose patrolled in slow, menacing circles. Its beak was the shade of orange that usually suggested poison, and its eyes, when fixed on Decimus, seemed to promise a future in which no one left with their dignity intact.

Near the chancel, the Scribe sat with his head bent over a scroll, lips moving in silent war with the words. He was a thin man in a robe two sizes too large, its sleeves stuffed with additional parchment for emergencies. The moment he saw the pair approach, his mouth compressed to a flat line.

"Visitors," he said, with a precision usually reserved for venomous reptiles. "State your claim."

Decimus repeated the story, adding, "The laurels were meant for the Triumph. The error was administrative, not intentional."

The Scribe sighed. "Nothing is ever intentional in this city. That's the problem." He gestured to a display niche behind the altar, where the laurel wreaths had been placed—upon the brow of a statue of Propheticus Minor, the city's patron of unresolved outcomes. In the statue's left hand, a scroll; in the right, a palm upraised in the international sign of 'let us wait and see.' The laurels themselves looked none the worse for their journey, but were now entwined with a streamer of purple silk and a chain of what appeared to be miniature dried fish.

"Once on the brow, always on the brow," said the Scribe. "To remove them now would require a full misinterpretation hearing, with witnesses, as previously noted."

"We're pressed for time," said Decimus. "Is there any alternative?"

The Scribe thought, then nodded to the goose. "Omen decides. If she allows you to approach, you may reclaim your wreath. If not—" he glanced at Gaius, whose attempt at stealth had brought him within pecking range "—you will leave, and reconsider the wisdom of poetic mandates."

Gaius backed up, hands raised in surrender. "I didn't mean to cause trouble. I just wanted to enhance the Triumph."

The Scribe made a noise of deep, academic derision. "Enhancement is the enemy of ritual."

Before Decimus could formulate an argument, a new voice echoed from the ambulatory: "Let them try. If the city is to be saved, it will not be by rules alone."

Licinia glided into view, barefoot, hair wild, eyes aglow with the conviction of a woman who had seen several futures and disliked them all. She wore a sash of ceremonial purple, upon which were pinned no less than four medals for "Excellence in Interpretive Ritual," two of which were self-awarded. A retinue of followers drifted after her, among them a girl with a tambourine and a boy who looked as if he had not slept in a week.

"Licinia," said the Scribe, tone icy with a history of mutual disappointment.

"Scribe," she replied, voice honeyed and unctuous, "always a pleasure to witness your dedication to form over substance."

She addressed Decimus. "You want the wreaths? Take them. But you must do it right. There is an order to things, even here."

Gaius brightened. "Is there a ritual?"

Licinia beamed. "There's always a ritual." She motioned her acolytes forward, who produced a flagon of wine and two battered cups.

"We'll settle this by the ancient method," she said. "Trial by Oracular Dance."

The Scribe buried his face in his hands. "Not again."

But there was no stopping it. The acolytes began to clear a space before the altar, the boy rolling up a mat and the girl arranging candles in a circle. Omen the goose, having seen this before, retreated to a safe distance.

Licinia poured the wine, filled the cups, and handed one to Decimus. "Drink," she commanded, "and open yourself to the will of the gods."

He hesitated. Gaius, not so burdened by caution, drained his own cup and immediately began to sway to the rhythm of the tambourine, which now sounded with increasing urgency.

Licinia raised her arms. "Let the question be clear: Who is worthy to bear the laurels?"

The acolytes joined hands, formed a ring, and began a slow rotation. Decimus sipped, coughed, then found himself being gently but irresistibly drawn into the circle.

Licinia's voice soared above the growing hum. "Let the omens speak. Let the answer come, not from lips, but from movement."

The tambourine's rhythm grew wild, then fractured. Gaius, caught up in the mood, attempted a pirouette, failed, and staggered into the Scribe's desk, sending a drift of parchment to the floor. The Scribe shrieked, more in horror than rage, and began gathering the sheets with the speed of the damned.

In the midst of this, Licinia stepped into the ring, her movements equal parts grace and calculated menace. She circled Decimus, eyes locked on his face. "Do you feel it?" she whispered.

He did, but could not name it. The incense, the thrum of feet on stone, the dizzying proximity of the laurel wreaths—it all blended into something not unlike dread.

Licinia extended a hand. "Take the wreath, Decimus. If you dare."

He reached for it, only to be intercepted by Omen, who hissed and snapped at his fingers.

Licinia laughed, the sound ringing with triumph. "The old gods still have bite."

Gaius, by now deeply inebriated, attempted to reason with the goose. "We only need a little laurel, for the good of the city. We'll put it back afterwards."

Omen was unconvinced.

The Scribe, seeing his chance, swept forward. "This is a mockery. The rules—"

Licinia stopped him with a look. "The rules serve the living, not the other way round."

She turned to Decimus. "If you want the laurels, you must offer something in return. That is the way of exchange."

He thought. "What do you want?"

Licinia smiled. "The truth. Give us your prophecy. The real one."

Decimus hesitated, then produced the strip of parchment he had found in the archives. The words glimmered in the candlelight:

One man will seize the crown. His cheekbones shall divide the people.

Licinia took the parchment, held it high. "This is what the gods demand. A future that can be known, yet never understood."

She handed the scroll to the Scribe, who examined it, then grudgingly nodded.

"Take the wreaths," he said, "and may the city survive your version of history."

Decimus bowed, retrieved the laurels from the statue, and backed away, wary of Omen, who had not relaxed her guard.

Licinia raised her cup. "To the new king of the Triumph," she intoned. The acolytes cheered, Gaius attempted another dance, and the Scribe resumed his seat, muttering about the decline of standards.

They left the Temple as the first light of dawn crested the city. Gaius, sobered by the cold, regarded the wreaths with awe. "We did it," he said. "We really did it."

Decimus was not so sure.

At the foot of the hill, a contingent of augurs waited, their faces a study in expectation and apprehension.

"Did you recover the laurels?" asked their leader.

Decimus presented them. "Intact and, I think, blessed by every force in Rome."

The augur nodded, then gestured to the others. "Begin preparations. The city will have its Triumph, after all."

As they walked away, Gaius nudged Decimus. "You know, I've never seen a ritual like that before. Do you think it actually worked?"

Decimus thought of the scroll fragment, its words etched into his memory. "It worked as well as anything does, here."

He watched the augurs process up the hill, laurels gleaming in the new day, and wondered if the city was prepared for the future it had just engineered.

Behind him, Omen the goose stood at the crest, silhouetted against the sky, wings outstretched as if embracing the uncertain dawn.

EIGHTEEN

If Lucilla Minor's private study had ever contained comfort, it was strictly for the benefit of auditors. The room was as much a bunker as a workspace, its windows bricked up in accordance with some old Republican security protocol and its furniture selected for the efficient transmission of back pain. Wall to wall, shelves sagged under the mass of legislative scrolls, case law, ledgers, and the odd set of wax tablets so brittle with age they were best approached with prayers and tongs. In pride of place, above the main desk, a gladius hung in a leather sheath, conspicuously unused and rumoured to have been an office-warming gift from a grateful ex-consul. Lucilla claimed it was decorative, but the blade was sharpened every Equinox, and she alone had the key to its lock.

At present, the desk served not as a writing surface but as a battlefield. Lucilla stood behind it, arms folded, back so straight it threatened to slice her toga in two. Before her, a phalanx of scrolls had been arrayed, their positions adjusted with the geometric precision of a general staging a siege. Candlelight danced on the waxed surface, casting flickering shadows of impending administrative doom.

Aulus and Decimus arrived at the threshold in tandem, both resembling men who had been chased by poultry and then trampled by a livestock parade. They were damp, soot-stained, and radiated an aroma of laurel, mildew, and desperate exertion. Decimus's hair had acquired an electric quality, the aftershock of his recent ritual humiliation, and Aulus's toga bore the ragged edge of an encounter with something sharper than embarrassment.

Gaius the Landlord sat on a bench to the side, feet up on a crate of surplus codices, humming a little tune and scribbling furiously on a blank scroll. He did not look up as the others entered, but his smile widened in anticipation of fresh disaster.

Lucilla said nothing. She pointed, with two fingers, to the strip of carpet before her desk—an unsubtle command.

Aulus obeyed first, shuffling forward, leaving a faint trail of ash and dignity. Decimus followed, clutching his satchel as though it might shield him from consequences.

"Well?" Lucilla said, her voice clipped and pitiless.

Aulus made a half-bow that suggested both apology and spinal misalignment. "The laurel is secured. There were... complications."

Lucilla fixed him with a stare so unblinking it might have been borrowed from the Justice bust on her shelf. "And?"

"The Prophetic Recalibration team resisted," Decimus supplied. "We performed the customary rites. There was a contest. The laurel is intact." He glanced sideways, as if daring Gaius to contradict him.

Gaius did not look up from his writing. "The goose was a nice touch," he said. "Very symbolic. I wrote a new stanza for the Triumph's hymn in its honour."

Lucilla's lips compressed, registering the information as both infuriating and inevitable. "And the delivery?"

"It's with the augurs," Decimus said. "They're preparing for the ceremony. The—" He struggled for a diplomatic term. "—incident has been contained."

Aulus shifted, attempting to wrest control of the narrative. "We did encounter one additional complication. The Temple Scribe has threatened to file a formal grievance over the conduct of the 'oracular contest'. Apparently the standard for wine consumption was exceeded."

Lucilla arched one eyebrow, as if conducting a mental inventory of all the crises currently in progress. "Let the Scribe file his grievance. I'll forward it to the Department of Regret. They're due for a backlog."

Aulus relaxed, just enough to remind everyone of his capacity for tension.

Decimus cleared his throat. "Is there a new directive? The parade team is... unsettled."

Lucilla reached for a scroll at the top of her array, unrolled it with the air of one unveiling a battle plan, and set her fingertips on the lines of script. "The situation has deteriorated. The City Council is split. The augurs are fighting over the sequence of omens, the Tribune is threatening to quarantine the entire Triumph, and Caesar himself has sent a letter suggesting that if the parade is further delayed, he may have to improvise a personal demonstration. With swords."

Gaius, now idly carving a doodle in the margin of his scroll, piped up: "We could always run the Triumph as scheduled, but replace all actual combat with interpretive dance. The city's never seen a phalanx waltz, and I think they'd enjoy the innovation."

Lucilla ignored this, or perhaps stored it for later blackmail. "Here is what will happen." She tapped the desk for emphasis. "The Triumph will proceed. But we will control the narrative, down to the last syllable. I have secured a writ from the Ministry of Moral Memory—"

Gaius let out a low whistle, the kind usually reserved for particularly ambitious tax audits.

"—which authorises us to prepare an official version of events prior to the parade itself." She eyed Decimus, who straightened in alarm. "You will write it."

Aulus blanched. "What, the whole parade? Before it happens?"

"Precisely," said Lucilla. "The actual event is irrelevant. What matters is what is remembered. If we can get the official scroll into circulation ahead of the spectacle, the city will believe whatever version we approve."

Decimus said, "But Caesar—"

"Will be too busy counting his own likenesses to notice," Lucilla interrupted. "The odes and hymns will be ready. Gaius—"

He looked up, beaming. "Yes, Senator?"

"—you will supply as many variations of the

Triumph's hymn as possible. Subtle changes only. Each designed to flatter a different audience. We want the plebeians to hear heroism, the patricians to hear tradition, and the augurs to hear the echo of their own voices."

Gaius's pen was already moving. "Should I add a section for the livestock? The city's invested in the animal component."

"Do it," Lucilla said. "The more plausible the detail, the less likely anyone will question the overall narrative."

Aulus, finding his courage in the bottom of some forgotten reserve, said, "This is... forgive me, but this is unprecedented. If anyone finds out—"

Lucilla sliced the air with a hand. "If anyone finds out, you refer them to me. If it works, you'll be lauded as a genius of process innovation. If it fails, I'll draft your apology myself and recommend early retirement on full salary."

Aulus opened and closed his mouth, then nodded, the movement that of a man stepping into his own grave out of politeness.

Lucilla turned to Decimus. "You'll start immediately. Use the parade's actual schedule as a template, but embellish. Focus on the themes of unity, renewal, and—" she glanced at her gladius, then back at Decimus, "— strategic obedience."

Decimus said, "And the prophecy?"

She shrugged. "The prophecy is what we say it is. If there's to be a donkey, let it symbolise modesty and the virtues of the common man. If there's to be a laurel, let it crown not just the victor, but the city itself. Take control of the symbols, and the mob will follow."

Gaius grinned, pleased at the prospect of a city-wide exercise in compulsory metaphor.

Aulus, pale but functional, asked, "And the smoke pots? The rigged carts? The children in animal costumes?"

Lucilla replied, "They stay. If you have a better distraction, implement it. But the more the crowds have to talk about, the less attention they'll pay to the parade's failings."

A tap at the door interrupted. None had heard it open, but now, in the space just inside the threshold, stood Domitia. She wore her work clothes, but somehow managed to project the aura of a woman about to stage a coup. Her arms were folded, her eyes amused.

"Did I miss the part where the city saves itself, or are we still in the preamble?" she asked.

Lucilla considered her for a moment, then said, "You have a contribution?"

Domitia stepped forward, hands open. "I have access to the costumes, the floats, and the entire staff of parade performers—many of whom would prefer to work for favours rather than coin. They're loyal to spectacle, not to any one master. If you want them to sing, they'll sing. If you want them to march backwards, they'll do that too. All they require is a plausible reason."

Aulus mumbled, "This is career suicide."

Domitia heard him. "Not if the city loves it. If it works, they'll write poems. If it fails, you'll be on the next float out of town, disguised as an amphora."

Lucilla nodded, slowly. "Good. You're in charge of deployment. Every costume, every actor, every donkey—

real or symbolic—goes through you. And you report only to me."

Domitia smiled, not without malice. "It's always a pleasure to report to a professional."

Gaius, ever the optimist, lifted his cup in salute. "To the new parade!"

There was a pause, the silence filling with the anticipation of disaster or triumph—either would suffice.

Decimus, feeling the weight of his assignment settle like a cold compress on his brain, said, "How soon do you want the first draft?"

Lucilla replied, "By dawn. If we get ahead of the story, nothing can stop us."

Aulus inhaled, as if about to say something memorable, then thought better of it. He nodded, gathered his papers, and turned to go.

Gaius followed, humming his hymn under his breath, the words already mutated beyond recognition.

Domitia lingered, regarding Lucilla with a mixture of suspicion and respect. "You really think you can outwit the city?"

Lucilla answered, "I don't have to. I only have to distract it until the real crisis passes. That's what government is."

Domitia accepted this, and slipped out the door.

Decimus hesitated, hand on his satchel. "If you need anything else—"

Lucilla fixed him with her gaze. "If I need anything, Flaccus, you'll be the first to know."

He bowed, awkward but sincere, and left.

Lucilla remained at her desk, fingers steepled, eyes on

the flickering candlelight. She considered the gladius on the wall, then the scrolls arrayed before her. The parade would be a disaster, of course. But it would be her disaster, and, if she played it right, the city would ask for an encore.

In the darkness of the study, she permitted herself a thin, unguarded smile.

Decimus walked beside Domitia, whose route through the quarter seemed neither random nor predetermined. She paused at each turning, as if sampling the air, and then advanced with a confidence that dared the cobbles to disagree. Rain threatened with every wind-shiver, but never quite committed. The wetness that clung to the stones was the accumulation of old weather and the city's own condensation, pooled in slick mirrors that doubled the world without improving it.

They spoke little at first. The night invited discretion, and the nearer they drew to Lucilla's neighbourhood the more eyes seemed to press from behind shutters, or from the gaps between laundry lines strung at throat height. Somewhere, a child howled the day's last complaint before being silenced by parent or fatigue.

Domitia broke the silence. "You realise," she said, voice low, "that your friend the Senator just declared war on half the city?"

"I suspected as much," Decimus replied, adjusting

his pace to match hers. "It's possible she declared war on all of it, but is only charging the rest by the hour."

Domitia grinned, the moon snagging on the tip of her canine. "They'll try to eat her alive. Or, failing that, they'll go for the next course." She glanced at him. "You're not the stringiest, but you're the most digestible."

He took this in stride, which was the only way to take it. "I never expected to reach dessert."

They passed through a small market square, deserted now but littered with the detritus of earlier trade. A crate of wilted chard, two wine amphorae rolling in the gutter, and, atop a plinth, a marble bust of a senator nobody remembered. Domitia stopped, studied the bust, and plucked a withered flower from the crack at its base.

She tossed the flower to Decimus. He caught it, barely. "For luck?" he ventured.

"For camouflage. If anyone asks, you're a romantic."

He tucked it behind his ear, where it flopped, tragic and unimpressive.

They walked on. In this stretch, the paving stones sloped towards the river, making every step an act of resistance. Domitia glanced over her shoulder, then said, "You know there's already a rumour going around that Brutus's head is being minted on coins."

"I'd heard," said Decimus, "but I assumed it was satire."

"They're making them in the Subura. Street currency, mostly, but if the city's in the mood for a new Caesar, it doesn't take much to change the face on the coin."

Decimus considered. "He'll never accept a crown."

"He won't have to. The city will wear it for him." She shrugged, which in her case seemed to encompass both shoulders and soul. "That's the other side of your Senator's plan. If she fails to hijack the narrative, someone else will. And you'll be first in line to explain it to the tribunals."

They entered a narrow corridor of lamp-lit homes, each with a different scent of dinner or quarrel leaking from its door. A drunk, slumped against a wall, lifted a hand in greeting as they passed, then let it fall, as though having remembered a reason to regret sobriety.

Decimus said, "Why are you telling me this?"

Domitia smiled, but it didn't last. "Because you're not half as clever as you think you are, and twice as clever as anyone wants you to be. The city hates a man who doesn't fit his paperwork."

They walked in silence for a block, shoes splashing through puddles that gleamed like the discarded eyes of statues.

Decimus broke the quiet. "Did you ever think it could be fixed? The Republic?"

She didn't answer immediately. At the end of the alley, they paused beneath an oil lamp. "No," she said. "But I thought it might at least be replaced with something less embarrassing."

He smiled, a bare showing of teeth. "I used to believe that the truth would make a difference. That if you put enough of it in the right order, it would crowd out the lies."

She laughed, not kindly. "That's how they keep you harmless. Make you believe the filing cabinet matters."

They reached a crossroads, where the road divided around a shrine so eroded by time and rainfall that only the faintest hint of divinity remained. Decimus halted, uncertain if they would part here or continue. Domitia faced him, close enough that he could smell the lye and citrus of her trade, overlaid with the faint tang of exhaustion.

She produced a small leather pouch from her sleeve and offered it to him.

He frowned, then took it. The pouch was old, scuffed, the drawstring knotted in a style he recognised from the archives. He undid it, more by memory than sight, and tipped the contents into his palm.

A seal stamp. Brass, cold, and heavy with implication. The official insignia of the Office of Official Histories—his office, his own missing seal, vanished some weeks prior and written off as a casualty of the city's entropy.

He turned it over in his hand, thumb tracing the shallow grooves of the emblem.

"Someone's been writing in your name," said Domitia. "You should see the letters I get. All very official. All very urgent."

He looked at her, seeking either explanation or accusation, but her face had retreated to the neutral mask she wore with strangers.

He said, "Why give it back to me?"

She shrugged. "I liked your version of events better than theirs." She stepped back, into the margin between lamp and dark. "Besides, if you're going to be a scapegoat, you should at least sign your own confession."

She turned to go, then paused. "You'll want to see the other thing in there."

He checked the pouch again. At the bottom, stuck to the seam, a single coin: new, silver, the head unmarked by history but recognisable all the same. The cheekbones were, if anything, even more pronounced than rumour.

He closed his fist around the pouch, the weight of the seal and the coin a warning and a promise. By the time he looked up, Domitia was gone, absorbed by the city's appetite for secrets and complications.

He made his way home, moving slower now, past the homes with their flickering lamps and the distant, invisible river. He knew what would come next: the forging, the scapegoating, the sudden collapse of loyalty when the wind changed. But for now, he walked, the official seal heavy in his pocket, the flower still drooping behind his ear, and the night holding its breath for the next version of the truth.

NINETEEN

The records chamber of the Office of Official Histories had acquired, in the night, an extra sign. The regular placard, which said simply "AUTHORIZED PERSONNEL ONLY," had been amended with a waxed tablet slotted above: "NOW HIRING: WILLING TO LIE?" This, Decimus Flaccus reflected, was the most honest statement the place had ever displayed. He entered, ducked the lintel, and found his "sub-committee for historical reinterpretation" arrayed precisely as predicted: Gaius the Landlord already making free with the wine, and Aulus Malleolus hunched over a scroll, copying from one version of events into another as if the process itself might generate a third, truer record by sheer friction.

Scrolls littered the trestle table, many with the official seal half-scraped off and the new seal, a crude likeness of Lucilla Minor's signet, pressed on in hasty wax. One entire stack had been condemned for "insufficient optimism," another for "potential interpretive mischief." The room was so full of crossed-out lines, footnotes, and stains of questionable origin that it resembled not a records office but the aftermath of a failed inquisition.

Decimus gave his satchel to the wall hook and took the centre stool, which was warmer than it should have been. "Progress?"

"Spectacular," said Gaius, who had already poured three cups and tasted all. "We've produced two alternate parades, one in which the Republic triumphs by virtue of its own self-critique, and another where the Triumph is so triumphant that it negates itself and the crowd disperses in polite silence. I favour the first, but Aulus claims the 'negation ending' tests better in focus groups."

Aulus, who always looked like a man being held hostage by his own scheduling, said, "It's not a matter of favour. If you present a contradiction to the public, they'll simply choose the version least likely to implicate themselves. It's basic self-interest. My job is to make sure the preferred version is available in at least three languages and five font sizes."

Decimus scanned the uppermost draft. The opening lines were an improvement over yesterday's effort, though the tendency towards excessive metaphor remained: "*Upon the day ordained, the people assembled as one body, yearning for the honeyed nectar of mutual regard, and lo, the city's heart did pulse anew with purpose.*" He considered the line, and, rather than comment, drew a line through "honeyed nectar" and substituted "watery soup." Closer to both the experience and the weather forecast.

Gaius noticed. "Censoring poetry again, Flaccus?"

"Correcting for inflation," Decimus said. "If you want the crowd to believe, you must let them taste the ash in the bread."

Aulus set down his stylus. "The Senator wishes the new version to 'elevate the shared values of the Republic over the cult of individual glory.' Her words. I can't imagine Caesar will appreciate the demotion."

"Caesar has his own version," said Decimus. "It's our job to make sure the official record is less dramatic but more widely distributed."

The door shuddered open, admitting a breeze and a messenger boy whose face had already acquired the first layers of future regret. He held out a scroll, and said, "Urgent, sir. From the Palace." The boy lingered, presumably awaiting coin or, failing that, a moment of human kindness.

Decimus handed him a wedge of cheese and waved him out.

He broke the seal, read, and set the scroll on the table. "Licinia's omens are to be included at the front of the ceremony. By order of the augurs' tribunal." He raised his gaze to Gaius, who by now had transferred his attentions from the wine to a plate of olives. "You're friends with Licinia. Any idea how she'll play this?"

Gaius considered. "Depends how much she's had to drink. If sober, she'll make it about the inevitable decay of all things. If not, she'll celebrate the victory of life over bureaucracy, and probably recommend the consumption of the city's reserves in a single night. Either way, there will be a speech."

"Good," said Decimus. "We can shape the narrative

to either outcome. If she predicts collapse, we note the city's resilience. If she predicts excess, we frame it as a deliberate act of civic therapy."

Aulus, who had started another column of numbers, said, "We're low on paper. If we continue at this rate, we'll have to use the backs of last year's condemnations."

Gaius perked up. "A palimpsest of failure. Very Roman. We can sell the idea to the Ministry as 'tradition'."

They set to work, Decimus dictating, Aulus recording, and Gaius adding colour commentary with the abandon of a man who had never once suffered from a shortage of adjectives. When the draft bogged down, as it inevitably did, Gaius would propose an interlude—a chorus of children, a symbolic untying of the city's "oldest knot," a parade of livestock adorned with the faces of the Senate's least photogenic members. Decimus rejected most, but kept a list for future emergencies.

At one point, Gaius suggested, "Why not cast the entire forum as a maiden, ripe for conquest by the returning hero?"

Decimus replied, "Because the forum, unlike a maiden, is already owned by half the city, and the other half is in litigation over visitation rights."

Aulus, stifling a laugh, said, "If we continue, we'll end up with a Triumph in which the only thing crowned is a goat and the rest of the city is in penance."

Gaius nodded, delighted. "That, my friend, is what they call satire."

They worked through the morning, the light

advancing up the wall in slow increments, the drafts piling ever higher. By midday, the table was a topography of revisions, each marked with a different colour of wax, the red for "approved," the green for "likely to incite riot," and the black for "destroy after reading."

Aulus uncorked a second jar of wine, this one labelled "Senatorial Quality." He poured for all, and for a moment, the three regarded their handiwork with the satisfaction of men who had wrestled chaos into submission, or at least pinned it beneath enough footnotes to discourage its escape.

Then the door opened again, this time admitting a messenger of a different order. The man was older, bearing the tunic and battered sandals of a retired municipal clerk, and carried an envelope sealed in blue—a rare shade, reserved for notices of potential treason or, occasionally, invitations to exclusive post-trial banquets.

Decimus took the envelope, cracked the seal, and read. His face, never much of a canvas, nonetheless managed a shade of pallor.

"Problem?" said Gaius, peering over the rim of his cup.

Decimus handed the letter to Aulus. "It's from Hortensius. The ex-archivist."

Aulus read aloud: *"The prophecy was altered. Check the second seal."*

For a moment, the room was quiet save for the sound of Gaius finishing his wine.

Decimus fetched from his satchel the copy of the prophecy they had obtained from the archives. The document, already infamous for its ability to destabilise any agenda, was rolled tight and banded with a fragment of ribbon, itself inscribed "Official Copy—Do Not Amend." He unrolled it, scanning the text, then held the page to the light.

A second, fainter script ran at an angle across the original: barely legible, but unmistakably the hand of a professional forger.

Aulus read, "*The first version was for the city. The second was for the victor.*"

Gaius, who understood nothing but the implications, said, "Brutus's version is not the public version."

Decimus nodded. "Which means someone has told him he's destined for the crown, while the official record will say otherwise."

Aulus, ever the administrator, said, "That's dangerous even for us."

Gaius, with uncharacteristic sobriety, said, "If the city finds out it's been promised two destinies, they'll split down the middle."

Decimus traced the line of red ink, then the line of regular ink, and understood—for the first time in his career—what it meant to be written out of one's own story.

He rolled the scroll, replaced the ribbon, and set it in the "to be burned" pile.

"Carry on," he said, his voice thin. "We have a parade to rewrite."

The others nodded, and the scratching of pens resumed, a counterpoint to the distant, thunderous preparation of the city for its next and possibly last great moment.

In the corridor outside, the "NOW HIRING" sign hung crooked, as if aware that even the most creative liars eventually ran out of ink.

TWENTY

The Via Triumphalis wore its hangover proudly. Overnight, the bunting had multiplied, now drooping in rich tatters from every window, statue, and the occasional stray goat. Early mist clung to the cobbles and to the citizens who lined them, most of whom had spent the last forty-eight hours in preparation for the event, and the last twelve undoing it with a mixture of local wine and elaborate gossip.

At the head of the avenue, the Senate's "Triumph of Triumphs" Committee had installed a platform of marble and resentment, upon which the city's most photogenic dignitaries posed with the solemnity of condemned art. Above them, banners unfurled, spelling out official slogans that had already been amended by sharp-eyed pranksters: "Caesar Brings Peace" now read "Caesar Brings Peas," with a cascade of painted legumes tumbling after.

The opening blast of ceremonial horns did not so much startle the crowd as it did the city's birds, which exploded from the Forum's statuary in a panic, circling the route in a series of omens that several augurs immediately began to interpret for a fee.

Caesar himself arrived not on foot, nor horseback, but in a chariot so gilded it was rumoured to have been forged from the melted dowries of three rival generals. His hair was arranged in the latest heroic style, his face oiled to an ambiguous shine, and his cloak so white it cast its own shadow. Flanking him were twelve attendants, each tasked with dabbing his brow, dusting his laurels, and, in the event of assassination, dying first.

To the trained observer, Caesar's expression was not one of triumph. It was the look of a man braced for either adulation or an unexpected audit.

Behind the chariot followed the floats: one bearing a reconstruction of the conquered East, another laden with jars of "Persian honey" (actually imported from Crete), and, toward the rear, a replica of the Golden Ledger of Civic Glory. This last was towed by a pair of donkeys, which, on arrival at the appointed starting line, immediately staged a sit-down. Nothing, not the offers of oats, nor the persuasive arguments of their handlers, nor the creative curses of a freelance exorcist, would budge them.

Aulus Malleolus, sweating through two layers of parade livery, appeared at the head of the float, clipboard in hand and veins in neck operating at unsafe pressure. "Flaccus!" he bellowed, gesturing for Decimus to approach. "We're behind schedule, the laurels are wilting, and the donkeys aren't following the script."

Decimus, who had already fielded three disasters

before breakfast, said, "Have you tried promising them a pension?"

Aulus said, "We offered them a statue. They ate it."

From the sidelines, Lucilla Minor regarded the scene through the calm, dark eyes of one who has seen enough parades to know the crowd is always on the verge of a better offer. She sat in the front rank of the senatorial platform, her toga crisp, her hands neatly gloved in white. On her lap, a folio bulged with last-minute amendments and the official text of the Triumph's ode, each marked with her own notes in surgical red.

At the main podium, Gaius the Landlord assumed his position as Master of Ceremonies. The man had washed, or at least perfumed, and now wore a toga with such excess of gold trim it might have been visible from the moon. He tapped the amplification crystal, cleared his throat, and addressed the assembly:

"O citizens! O inheritors of seven hills and, as of today, several new provinces! We are gathered to bear witness to Rome's greatest hour—"

He paused, either for effect or to collect a scrap of dignity. The crowd responded with the uncertain cheer of people unsure whether their jobs depended on it.

"In this Triumph, we do not merely celebrate the victories of the sword, but the conquests of the spirit—" Here, Gaius faltered, eyes flicking to the scroll he held. For a heartbeat, the silence thickened.

He began to read, at first in a steady if perfunctory cadence. "Let the laurel crown the worthy, and let the city rejoice in her new peace—"

On the platform, Lucilla nodded at the precise moment her notes indicated.

Gaius continued, but now his quill-hand shook, and the words began to drift:

"Let the victor's brow bear the green of hope, unless the victor's heart bear the black of ambition. Let Rome beware of the man who wears two faces, and let no cheekbone rise above its station..."

Aulus, still wrestling the donkeys, glanced up, realising the script had gone off-piste.

"Let no Triumph be so great that it cannot be outlived by its own rumour. For the only true glory is that which does not need a parade—"

Gaius's voice rose, acquiring a timbre that made several matrons fan themselves and three junior clerks take notes for posterity.

"Let the laurels wither, if the city thrives. Let the greatest among us remember: the day is short, but the night is long, and the crowd will remember what the victors forget."

By now, Lucilla had shifted in her seat, the lines of her mouth compressing in appraisal. A senator at her side muttered, "That's not in the official version." She silenced him with a glance.

In the pit, Aulus resorted to manual propulsion, bracing his shoulder against the Golden Ledger float while Decimus barked orders to anyone with arms. The donkeys, now committed to inertia, had to be dragged by a gang of street urchins pressed into service at a sesterce per head. The float lurched forward, only to catch on a paving-stone, sending the leading jar of Persian honey into the air and onto the head of a passing augur.

Up above, the crowd watched this not as a failure, but as the sort of spectacle they had been promised all along. Vendors hawked burnt nuts and olives from baskets, occasionally pelting one another for the crowd's amusement. The stench of overripe grapes and mutton competed with the incense of the temples, with neither side winning.

Back at the podium, Gaius, now fully possessed by the Muse or his own sense of theatre, leaned in:

"Behold the man who claims to conquer the world, yet cannot conquer himself! Behold the city, whose true conqueror is not on this route but in every whisper and every home—"

Aulus, having finally achieved motion, made frantic throat-cutting gestures at Gaius, but the crowd, at first perplexed, now began to follow along, repeating snatches of the oration:

"Laurels wither! Cheekbones beware! The night is long—!"

A splatter of honeyed augur struck a priest in the eye, who, being a professional, instantly declared it an omen of impending clarity. Word spread like syrup through the crowd, which now pressed closer to the floats, eager to see the next mishap.

Caesar, in his chariot, maintained composure only by force of will and an occasional sip from a flask disguised as a sceptre. The first time he attempted a wave, he was pelted with a handful of peas, which clung to the oil on his arm like green warts. He ignored this, instead focusing on the great arch ahead, where the final leg of the parade would elevate him from spectacle to legend, or, if the current trajectory held, to punchline.

At the rear, the float of "Innovations and Virtues" had lost its accompanying dancers, who, upon noticing the crowd's preference for Gaius's impromptu lines, abandoned their routine and joined the chant. Decimus, pinned between his clipboard and the mass of failed logistics, realised he could do nothing but ride the collapse to its conclusion.

The avenue now thrummed with competing versions of the day's meaning. Some clung to the official schedule, mouthing the approved odes as they passed. Others, infected by Gaius's spirit, shouted the new prophecy at every passing dignitary. By the time the column reached the temple steps, the crowd had tripled in size and halved in restraint.

Lucilla, watching the spectacle, allowed herself the briefest of smiles. "The best-laid plans," she murmured.

Aulus, red-faced, made his way to the side of the platform, where he was immediately cornered by two women from the Ministry of Moral Memory, both of whom wanted to know whether the parade was on time, on message, and whether the donkeys could be retroactively edited from the record.

Gaius, at the conclusion of his speech, stepped down from the podium to thunderous applause, half of which was likely for the promise of a lunch break. He was immediately mobbed by a group of poets who wished to buy him a drink and steal his best lines.

In the midst of the chaos, Decimus found himself

standing alone, clipboard cracked, float abandoned. He looked down at the honey on his hands, then up at the city beyond the arch. In that moment, it occurred to him that the day was not a triumph for anyone, but that, in a way only Rome could manage, it had transcended all plans to become something else: a monument to survival, to improvisation, to the enduring power of utter, irredeemable mess.

And as he watched, the last of the bunting sagged to the ground, where a goat immediately ate it.

The parade, for all its flaws, was a success.

The city would remember it forever, or at least until the next disaster.

The Temple of Jupiter had never been more ablaze with expectation, or more obviously unfit for it. Each step of the grand staircase was occupied: priests in ceremonial gold, senators in bleached togas so stiff they rustled with every motion, and, behind them, the day's survivors—citizens crammed shoulder to shoulder, still sticky with honey and waiting to see whether the city's luck would finally expire.

In the portico, the air was thick with the perfume of incense, and whatever the city's wind had last collected from the refuse pits. The marble glared, the gods glared back, and the goose, imported for ritual but now clearly on loan to chaos, pecked methodically at a deacon's sandals. No one had the will to stop it.

At the centre of it all, Caesar ascended the steps, cloak streaming, hair re-glossed to perfection. The crowd, at first hesitant, now roared him on with the conviction of people determined not to appear undecided.

The climax began, as all climaxes did, with a speech. The High Priest, voice echoing off every polished column, invoked the gods, the ancestors, and the city's indestructible moral fibre. He then called for the laurel, and for a moment, the assembly held its collective breath.

A team of ceremonial assistants, robed in the silver and indigo of the Festival Guild, advanced bearing the Laurel Chest of Glory.

They set the box on a plinth. The High Priest intoned the formula. He undid the seven symbolic locks, each click echoing in the hush. He opened the lid.

Nothing.

A gasp, or rather, a thousand gasps in harmony.

The box was not just empty; it was clean. Not a sprig, not a leaf, not even the consolation dust of prior laurels.

For a heartbeat, no one moved.

Then the High Priest, a veteran of six civic crises and three scandals, clapped the box shut and fainted backwards into the arms of his subdeacons. It was a faint worthy of legend: slow, stately, and engineered for maximum sympathy. The crowd responded with appropriate awe. Two children at the front began to cry. A street vendor offered odds on whether he'd wake up before lunch.

Caesar looked to the crowd, then to the chest, then, at last, to the Senate's platform. His eyes, even oiled, managed to signal a depth of betrayal for which Latin had only recently invented a word. For a moment, he seemed ready to improvise. He gripped the edge of the plinth, seeking a line, a gesture, some last reserve of dignity.

He found none.

Instead, Lucilla Minor stood, and with the ease of one stepping into her own legend, raised her right hand. The crowd, by now primed for any excuse to change focus, gave her silence.

She spoke, not with the oratory of a candidate but the flat, clear tone of a woman more accustomed to verdicts than rhetoric.

"This is an omen," she said. "Rome will not crown one man an emperor while the Republic still breathes."

The line, already perfect, hung in the air just long enough for it to become historical. The crowd, unsure, looked from Lucilla to the box, then to Caesar, whose face now resembled the glaze on a day-old tart. After a moment, a smatter of applause. Then, as always, the city's mood veered on a coin: what began as tentative clapping swelled into a full-throated ovation.

Lucilla remained standing. She offered Caesar the smallest, most surgical of bows. He accepted it with a nod, then turned to his attendants, who now, in absence of laurel, hastily unfurled a banner that read "The Republic Endures!" The banner had clearly been made for emergencies, its corners frayed and its script too large for the occasion, but it sufficed.

Below the steps, Aulus Malleolus and Gaius the Landlord conferred, faces close. "Did you authorise that line?" whispered Aulus, panic threatening his grip on the day's reality.

Gaius, who had long since stopped caring, replied, "I gave her the opening. She found the ending."

Further down, Decimus Flaccus watched the scene as a scribe might watch a building collapse: a mixture of horror, admiration, and the grim certainty that he'd be blamed for the rubble. His clipboard, once a shield, now felt like evidence.

He looked up in time to see Licinia.

She emerged from the crowd not as a prophet, nor as a performer, but as herself: barefoot, hair wild, eyes alight with the conviction of one who has anticipated every outcome and learned to love the messiest. She wore, over her robe, a necklace of dried olives and what appeared to be a feather boa, either symbolic or acquired during the procession.

She advanced to the front, paused at the foot of the stairs, and then began to chant—not in the measured, ceremonial voice of the official script, but in the ululating, half-mad cadence of the city's original language:

"The cheekbones! The cheekbones! Let them rise— let them rise! Rome shall be ruled by the man with the face of a god, and the hunger of a donkey—"

The crowd, uncertain, laughed, then joined in. A boy near the altar let out a donkey bray, which was answered, to the city's delight, by the real thing: Flamey, the parade's resident donkey, who, having escaped his post, now charged up the stairs, dragging behind him the ceremonial curtain and a boy clinging for dear life to its hem.

The effect was instantaneous. The donkey, startled by Licinia's gesticulations, veered sideways, knocking over a row of acolytes. The curtain wrapped around the base of the plinth, toppling it. The Laurel Chest of Glory crashed to the pavement, spilling not laurels, but a false pinewood bottom and a hundred tiny coins stamped with Brutus's profile.

The crowd surged, either to collect the coins or to avoid the donkey. Priests shouted, dignitaries ducked, and the banner—now caught in the wind—wrapped itself around the head of the High Priest, who had only just regained consciousness.

And then, as if to draw a line under the day, a pigeon descended from the temple's pediment and landed, with perfect aim, atop Caesar's head. It settled there, indifferent to the uproar, and began to preen.

For a moment, no one moved.

Then Gaius, who alone had been waiting for the punchline, shouted, "Most auspicious!" and the laughter rolled down the steps, through the crowd, and out into the city.

At the top, Lucilla watched it unfold, the satisfaction in her eyes muted but unmistakable. She reached into her sleeve, extracted a strip of parchment, and handed it to Aulus.

He read it, and his mouth, unused to surprise, dropped open.

She said, "Prepare the minutes. The Republic will want a full account."

He nodded, then, as an afterthought, asked, "What of the prophecy?"

Lucilla glanced at the coins littering the steps, at the

pigeon, at the donkey—now being led away by a delegation of laughing children—and at the city, which had already begun to debate the meaning of every detail.

She smiled. "Let them write their own."

At the base of the stairs, Decimus watched the city reclaim its story. He felt, at first, a pang of loss—years of work, endless revisions, a lifetime spent trying to control the narrative, all undone by a handful of animals and the world's least dignified omen.

But as the crowd dispersed, each carrying away their own version of the day, he understood that this had always been the point. History, like laurel, was made to wither.

He picked up a coin, turned it over, and slipped it into his pocket. Tomorrow, he would be asked to document the events; tonight, he resolved to remember them as they were.

Above, the pigeon shifted, then took flight, leaving Caesar's head bare at last.

The city, unburdened, began to celebrate.

And so, the day ended, not with the triumph of one man, but of the city itself, cheekbones to the sky, grinning at the possibility of yet another story.

TWENTY-ONE

Decimus arrived at the Senate courtyard at the hour when most men of ambition took their breakfast or their bribes. Today, the olive trees lining the approach had dropped more than their usual quota of fruit, as if in anticipation of a particularly slippery day. He made a note, not for the record, but for later: "Increase municipal olive-picking. Potential hazard." It would never be actioned.

The courtyard should have been bristling with clerks, runners, and the odd detachment of ceremonial guardsmen pretending to keep order. Instead, it was deserted but for Lucilla, who stalked its circumference with a velocity that threatened the edges of her own shadow. Her face was set to "audit," her hands folded behind her back as if to keep them from wringing each other into a confession.

Decimus paused a safe distance away, caught between the desire to call out and the certainty that this was a bad idea. Lucilla did not so much turn as swivel, her whole body rotating on the axis of willpower. She fixed him with the stare reserved for late reports and failed subordinates.

"You're late," she said, though the sun had not yet breached the top step.

"I'm early," he replied, because the only way to survive Lucilla's approach was to contradict it gently.

She allowed him a margin of truth. "You're less late than the others. I suppose that's progress."

They stood together for a moment, the silence compounded by the absence of the city's usual self-commentary. Even the birds seemed to have migrated for the day. Decimus wondered if word had gotten out.

The doors to the anteroom creaked open, admitting Tribune Scaevola and a cloud of powdered chalk. The Tribune wore the sort of expression that, in livestock, preceded a stampede or a sudden reversal of the digestive process.

"Lucilla," said Scaevola, offering Lucilla the professional nod of equals who despised their circumstances only slightly less than each other. "Flaccus." He greeted Decimus with the added weight of having remembered his name, which in Rome was the most reliable sign of friendship.

Scaevola carried a bundle of budget scrolls, the majority of which looked as if they'd been through three consecutive wars and a plague. He unrolled the top one with the care of a man diffusing a known but unscheduled explosive.

"These don't make sense unless someone's planning a

coup or an opera," he said, and spread the scrolls across the nearest bench.

Lucilla bent over the figures, her eyes tracking each line with the precision of a predatory bird evaluating a nest for weakness. "Explain," she said, in a tone that suggested he had exactly one chance.

Scaevola traced a column with his ink-stained finger. "Three days ago, the Civic Improvement Fund made a withdrawal of seventy thousand sesterces—ostensibly for road repairs. But the actual roadwork was contracted to the same consortium who managed the Laurel Disbursement, and the Laurel account shows a deficit, not a surplus. It's a double-spend, disguised by creative line items."

Decimus glanced at the totals. "But the laurel was delivered, was it not?"

Scaevola permitted himself a dry smile. "Delivered, yes. Applied, no. The physical laurels are in the temple, but the money that should have paid for them is still circulating. Meanwhile, the guards are being rotated on an 'emergency footing,' and someone has paid a premium to have every single painter in the city redecorate the Curia chamber. Overnight."

Lucilla closed her eyes, massaged the bridge of her nose, and exhaled through her teeth. "And?"

Scaevola shrugged. "On its own, it's just embezzlement. But the redundancy—the backups to the backups, the duplicated guard details, the contradictory schedules —it reads less like theft and more like rehearsal."

He let the word hang. Decimus, unused to being ahead of the curve, caught its implication immediately.

"You think the Senate's being set up for... what? A staged emergency?"

Scaevola gestured at the empty courtyard. "When's the last time you saw this place without a single loitering informant?"

Decimus tried to recall, and failed.

Lucilla opened her eyes, now unreadable. "You're both missing the point. Someone doesn't care about the money, or the ceremony, or even the optics. They want the stage. They want every Senator in one place, at one hour, with no one on the streets to see what happens next."

She turned to Decimus. "Has the poetry reached you yet?"

He blinked. "Only the usual. Doggerel and doomsaying."

She considered, then said, "The latest couplets are getting inventive. They call today the 'Ides of Surprise.' And there's a rumour the augurs refused to enter the Curia this morning. They're claiming a bad reading from the livers of the sacrificial bull."

Decimus muttered, "Typical. When the liver's bad, blame the animal."

But he felt the chill anyway, and it was not the hour.

Scaevola straightened, the motion causing three sheets of figures to slide to the floor. "Here's the last thing. The schedule for today's meeting isn't for budget review, or military oversight, or any of the usual. It's listed as 'Advisory Session: State of the Republic—All Members Required.' And it's signed off by—" He checked the bottom of the scroll. "—Caesar himself."

Lucilla folded her arms, the pose a challenge to fate. "If you want to stop it," she said to Decimus, "this is your last chance."

He made a sound—half protest, half incredulity. "Stop what?"

She regarded him with the pity she usually reserved for blind kittens and the more optimistic gladiators. "Whatever it is that's about to happen."

He felt his knees soften, as if the city's entire weight had suddenly migrated to his lower half. The world, even when off kilter, had always kept its imbalances at a polite distance. Now they were converging at the tip of a single olive branch.

He opened his mouth to answer, but the decision was made for him.

Domitia stepped into the courtyard, as if conjured by the collective dread. She wore the same apron as always, but it was speckled today with something darker than wine, and her hands were folded in front of her, innocent and terrifying.

"Too late," she said, with the calm of a woman breaking the news of a cancelled wedding. "They're already inside."

All eyes turned.

Scaevola said, "How do you know?"

Domitia's gaze flicked to Decimus, then to Lucilla, then back to the ground. "The Senator's wife sent me for urgent laundering. Only there is no wife. There's no Senator. There's only a roomful of men in their best togas, and half the ushers have swapped uniforms. No one's speaking. Not even the staff."

Lucilla swore, a rare and exotic flower in her garden of restraint.

Decimus found his voice. "And the weapon?"

She smiled, not kindly. "The real daggers were delivered an hour ago, tucked in the bottom of a basket of novelty cheese wheels. The first set failed quality inspection. You don't want to know how I know."

He absolutely did not.

Lucilla said, "Do you have a plan?"

Domitia shrugged. "If I did, it would be too late for that, too."

The sky had shifted in the time they'd been talking, and now it pressed down, low and thick. Somewhere in the city, a bell rang out of sequence, then fell silent. The only other sound was the distant, irregular clatter of a street vendor's cart, coming and going on the whim of the wind.

Scaevola began to gather up the budget scrolls, his hands moving faster than the rest of him. "We should warn—"

"—who?" said Lucilla. "No one listens until the obituary is published."

Decimus found himself moving before he realised it, not quite running, but accelerated by the inevitability of disaster. He reached the steps to the Curia at the same instant that the first of the disguised guards peeled off to intercept him. He recognised the man—twice recommended for demotion, never quite dismissed, always at the centre of bad paperwork and worse luck. The sort of man who would be last in the queue for loyalty, and first in the queue for a well-paying side.

Decimus pulled up, panting, and tried to step around.

The guard smiled, just enough to show that this, too, was a job. "In a hurry, sir?"

"I'm needed inside," Decimus said, with a desperation that surprised even him.

The guard examined his satchel, his shoes, his face, in that order. "A lot of people are," he replied, then, with unexpected gentleness, let him pass.

Decimus stumbled into the vestibule, barely clearing the threshold before another uniform appeared at his side, this one more nervous and less practiced. "Straight through," the second guard said, voice shaking. "They're waiting for you."

He was ushered into the main chamber, where the light was at once too bright and not bright enough. The benches, usually occupied by Senators and their hangers-on, were full but silent. Every man there was wrapped in his own layer of expectation. On the dais, an empty chair. To its left, the ledger of state; to its right, a ceremonial sword, unsheathed and gleaming.

Decimus scanned the room for Caesar, found him standing off to one side, deep in conversation with three men whose faces he'd only seen in the margins of official reports. Caesar's expression was at ease. Not the forced calm of a politician, but the easy restfulness of a man who had spent the morning in the company of angels and was now prepared to meet their opposites.

Brutus sat three rows back, hunched and trembling, a man rehearsing his own obituary. Cassius paced at the rear, arms folded, eyes flicking from Caesar to the exits as if scoring each for quality of escape.

The room's murmur quieted as Decimus advanced to the clerk's podium. He tried to read the faces, but found only the blankness of men rehearsing their own last lines.

He unslung his satchel, which now felt heavier than lead, and fumbled for the documents Lucilla had given him. He opened his mouth to speak, but the words deserted him.

He saw, in the periphery, Lucilla enter the chamber, Scaevola a step behind, Domitia nowhere but everywhere.

Caesar regarded Decimus with a flick of his gaze, then smiled as if amused by a late addition to the cast. He raised a hand, palm out, a gesture meant to silence, but it radiated condescension.

"Flaccus," he said, rolling the syllables like dice. "You're just in time. I was about to explain the necessity of... continuity."

Decimus's mouth moved, but the words hung, useless, in the hot air.

Caesar resumed, voice lazy but clear. "It has come to my attention that the city is plagued by disorder. That Rome, for all her glory, lacks the will to finish what she begins. I would see this rectified. Permanently."

The last word landed like a verdict. Several senators

shifted in their seats, their discomfort almost synchronised.

Cassius, unable to contain himself, barked a phrase that was meant to sound noble but landed somewhere south of desperation: "Sic semper tyrannis!" The line cracked on the last syllable, echoing up into the painted dome.

A ripple ran through the chamber. Every senator looked to every other, waiting for the necessary courage to manifest. Brutus stood, shaky, then sat again. A senator near the front dropped his stylus, the clatter so sharp that even the statue seemed to wince.

Caesar looked to the exits. The path was open; he could have run. Instead, he drew a breath, rolled his eyes as if at a child's prank, and waited.

It was Cassius who broke the standoff, striding down the aisle, his steps ringing loud and hollow. He reached Caesar, stopped, and for a heartbeat they stood together—opponent and target, old allies reunited in the city's favourite pastime. Cassius drew a blade from beneath his toga; it caught the lamplight, flashed, and for an instant, the room was so silent that Decimus could hear his own heartbeat and, beneath it, the faint wet shuffle of the janitor outside, already preparing for the clean-up.

Cassius raised the knife.

It was not a tidy job. The first thrust hit cloth, the second struck Caesar's arm, the third—guided by desperation—found flesh. Caesar grunted, then turned to Brutus, who now rose, as if tugged by a string, and advanced with a knife of his own. His hands shook so hard the blade wagged, and when he lunged, he nearly missed entirely.

The rest of the senators followed, some half-hearted, others with the resigned professionalism of men paying off a very old debt.

And then, in a manoeuvre not covered in any history of Rome, a pigeon, grown bold from a diet of parade confetti and bureaucracy, swooped through the open window and landed, with unerring aim, square on Decimus's head.

He ducked, but not in time, and stumbled forward, the pigeon flapping, the chamber erupting, the city's fate unspooling like a banner from the highest point of the Capitol.

He ran toward the centre of the commotion, scrolls flying from his arms, toga catching on the edge of the podium. He heard Lucilla's voice, loud and clear:

"If you're going to do it, Flaccus, now's the time!"

But Decimus, face plastered by feathers and fear, did the only thing he knew how. He picked up the first thing that came to hand—a ceremonial laurel wreath, intended for the day's victor—and, with a speed and accuracy born of total ignorance, hurled it into the fray.

It landed, perfectly, on the head of the nearest conspirator, who, startled by the coronation, dropped his dagger and fell backwards into the arms of his intended victim.

The rest, as always, happened at once.

For a moment it was less a murder than a slapstick. Men collided. Robes snagged. A sleeve caught fire on a ceremonial torch and the owner, refusing to miss his turn, stabbed at Caesar while patting out the flames with the other hand. At last, the man himself, blood now darkening the purple, fell to his knees at the foot of Pompey's statue, and looked up.

At the back, Domitia caught Decimus's eye and mouthed something he couldn't read. Later, he would decide it was, "Told you so."

Caesar was not quite dead. He bled, certainly—no legend could exaggerate the extent—but his eyes were still sharp, and, as he collapsed, they locked with Decimus's.

He bared his teeth, less in pain than in a last, defiant grin.

"Et tu?" said Caesar. The words were meant for Brutus, but it was Decimus who heard them.

He tried to reply, but the language failed him.

Caesar coughed, blood flecking his lips. "I warned you, Flaccus," he said, his voice already lower, already pulling away from the world. "You should've rewritten the ending."

He exhaled, sagged, and lay still. The silence that followed was so complete it seemed to press the chamber in on itself.

For several seconds, no one moved. Then, as if shaken from a trance, the senators retreated, melting from the chamber in twos and threes, each desperate to be the first to begin their version of events.

Cassius, splattered and wild-eyed, wiped his blade on the fallen man's cloak, then vanished.

Decimus pressed forward, tripped over the pigeon, and found himself face to face with the man who, of all the Senate, had seemed the least likely to be a part of anything dramatic: Brutus.

Brutus, bloodied but not bowed, looked at Decimus with the astonishment of a man seeing himself in a distorting mirror. He opened his mouth to speak, but Decimus, lacking any plan, simply handed him the dropped laurel.

"History will remember you for this," he said, though whether as murderer or saviour, he could not say.

Brutus took the wreath, confusion momentarily eclipsing his sense of destiny, and then, with a sigh, lowered himself to the marble floor and wept.

Decimus stood, the echoes of the disaster swirling around him like so much dust.

The pigeon, finally dislodged, flew up and perched atop the statue of Rome herself, unblinking and, for once, utterly silent.

He looked down at his hands, which were empty except for the splinters of laurel and the faint imprint of destiny.

Lucilla appeared at his side, her face a mixture of triumph and defeat. "Well," she said, "I suppose that's one version."

He nodded, unable to speak.

"Write it up, Flaccus," she said, turning away. "Make it better in the retelling."

And so ended the last day of the Republic: not with a speech, or a battle, or even a plan, but with a shrug, a pool of blood, and the knowledge that next week, the city would need another parade.

TWENTY-TWO

The annex room assigned to Decimus Flaccus had all the charm of an abandoned tomb and roughly twice the dust. In the pale hour after dawn, the light fought to enter through three hand-widths of dirty window, succeeded only in painting a dim rectangle on the opposite wall, and then gave up. The room had been intended, by its original designer, as a quarantine for records deemed "potentially hazardous to public morale." By the present day, it served as both archive and oubliette for the entire spectrum of failed narratives: half-burned scrolls, sheaves of parchment still stained with the blood of their former custodians, and a legion of forms marked in red "TO BE REWRITTEN IN LIGHT OF RECENT EVENTS." Dust floated in the air, and on the bench opposite Decimus, a junior scribe had collapsed into a nap so deep it bordered on self-preservation.

Decimus himself had yet to change out of the toga he had worn to the Curia the previous day. The lower hem was crisped brown and stiffer than the rest, a reminder of where he had kneeled, briefly, in the aftermath. The dried blood, his own or otherwise, had begun to flake, and whenever he shifted, the debris added another layer to the archaeological record accumulating on the flagstones. He had tried, earlier, to brush it away, but the gesture had only made things worse. He let his hands rest in his lap, ink-stained fingers curled like claws.

The first hour passed in silence, save for the scribe's intermittent snoring and the distant, methodical shriek of a whetstone being drawn across steel. At some point, Decimus considered joining the scribe in unconsciousness, but the inside of his eyelids only projected fresher and more intimate versions of yesterday's events. He resolved to stay awake, if only out of spite.

At the second hour, Supervisor Calvus arrived, or, more accurately, staged an entrance. He swept into the room with a confidence that owed much to the toga he wore—a dazzling specimen of municipal blue, every pleat pressed and arrow-straight, the neckline dusted with just enough white ash to suggest that Calvus had spent the morning "putting out fires" in the service of the Republic.

"Flaccus!" he called, as if the room were crowded and Decimus might have been lost among the furniture.

"Supervisor," Decimus replied, rising only as far as was strictly necessary.

Calvus surveyed the room, sniffed, and located the napping scribe with a precision that betrayed both long practice and a healthy disrespect for the junior ranks.

He snapped his fingers. "Boy! Out." The scribe roused, blinked, and bolted, scrolls tumbling to the floor in his wake.

Calvus smiled at the empty space, then closed the door behind him with the soft finality of a man sealing an evidence locker. He regarded Decimus as one might regard a piece of fruit in the process of going off.

"I trust you've had a moment to recover from yesterday's... spectacle?"

Decimus said, "The opportunity for reflection has been bountiful."

"Good, good." Calvus steepled his fingers. "You are aware, I trust, that Rome will require a new version of the facts."

It was not a question. Decimus considered for a moment how best to answer, decided against honesty, and settled for, "Of course."

Calvus beamed, revealing the off-white teeth of a man who never paid for his own dentistry. "The transition team is meeting at noon to coordinate messaging. Our preliminary polling indicates a strong public appetite for stability, and an even stronger appetite for avoiding blame. I am, therefore, authorising you to begin drafting the official record of Caesar's death. Please ensure it is equal parts tragic, inspiring, and ambiguous regarding the identity of the assailants." He paused, as if expecting applause, then added, "Oh, and leave yourself out of it."

Decimus said, "Of course, Supervisor."

"Excellent!" Calvus made a show of glancing at the parchment on the table, but did not touch it. "I'll have Hortensius bring you the latest source materials. Try not to get ahead of the narrative. If you require guidance, consult the attached theme sheet." He produced, from a sleeve, a single wax tablet, upon which was inscribed, in large and patronising script: "UNITY. RENEWAL. PERSONAL SACRIFICE."

Decimus accepted the tablet, which was already sticky with the sweat of previous briefings. "Understood."

Calvus clapped him on the shoulder, then on the other, as if confirming that Decimus was neither an impostor nor a cleverly disguised crate. "I have every confidence," he said, and left, the door closing with the faintest sigh of relief.

The silence returned. Decimus let his head rest in his hands for a moment, then reached for a quill. He stared at the blank scroll before him, the fibres wavering in the morning's first real draught. He could feel the weight of the city above, pressing down through the floors, the layers of history, the generations of men and women who had all believed, at one point, that the record could be made to reflect the truth.

I could write it exactly as it happened, he thought.

They would burn it before the ink dried, he thought.

He was still contemplating the mechanics of self-incrimination when the door creaked open and Hortensius entered, preceded by a half-dozen folders and followed by a faint but persistent smell of bad wine and desperation. Hortensius set the folders on the table with the care of a man handling either explosives or very old cheese.

"Flaccus," he said, voice raw with the effort of remaining professional, "I bring you the latest from the Ministry."

Decimus said, "Is any of it accurate?"

Hortensius considered, then said, "Some of it is more accurate than the rest."

He opened the first folder. "This one is from an eyewitness who claims that Caesar's last words were, and I quote, 'Et tu, Flaccus?'"

Decimus blinked. "That's not—"

"I know," said Hortensius. "But the witness was a Senator's nephew, and the nephew is now in charge of the Committee for Accurate History. I would recommend including it as a footnote, or perhaps as a rumour."

Decimus made a noncommittal noise.

Hortensius opened the second folder. "This is a circular from the Temple of Juno, asserting that the assassination was divine retribution for unpaid tithes."

"Do the gods accept murder as payment now?" Decimus asked.

"Apparently only on festival days. There's an asterisk." Hortensius moved on.

The third folder was thinner, but carried the unmistakable seal of the new Regime. "This is from the office of the Dictator's widow, Calpurnia. She suggests that Caesar's last request was for the city to remember him as a lover of peace, a patron of the arts, and a friend to all small animals."

"Wasn't he allergic to cats?" Decimus said.

"Only the ones that didn't vote for him," Hortensius replied, with a straight face.

The final folder was empty, save for a single page, upon which was written in a shaky but legible hand: "None of this is true. You know it, I know it, and so does everyone else. Write it anyway." The page was unsigned.

Decimus pushed the folders away. "I think I have enough."

Hortensius, for the first time that morning, sat down. He produced from within his toga a flask, unstoppered it, and offered it to Decimus. "It's not good," he warned, "but it's strong."

Decimus hesitated, then took a swallow. It tasted like a week in exile, but it did the job.

They sat together in the dust, the room slowly brightening as the sun, against all odds, found a way in.

Hortensius said, "Do you ever think about what happens to the records, after?"

"They get filed, or lost, or burned. Sometimes all three."

Hortensius nodded. "That's what I thought."

They sat a while longer. Hortensius offered the flask again, and this time Decimus did not hesitate.

After a time, Hortensius rose and gathered the folders, careful not to disturb the growing pile of ash accumulating near the hearth. He said, "You'll let me know if you want to change the ending."

Decimus said, "Does it ever work?"

"Not once," Hortensius said, and left.

Decimus was alone again. The room was warmer now, and the dust had thinned, replaced by a low, golden light that made even the piles of failed paperwork look almost distinguished.

He uncapped his inkwell, dipped his pen, and considered, for a moment, the possibility of writing nothing at all. He could simply leave the scroll blank, a monument to the truth that had so completely escaped the city.

But in the end, he began to write.

He started, as he always did, with a lie:

"Upon the dawn of the first day of the New Era, the people of Rome awoke to find themselves free."

He paused, read it back, and amended: "freer than yesterday."

He smiled, thin and crooked, and wrote on.

Above him, the city exhaled, the birds returned, and the morning went on as if nothing at all had happened.

In the far corner of the laundry, a shrine had been constructed of soap, twine, and the sort of votive candles favoured by people hedging their bets. Whether the effigy at its centre was intended to resemble Caesar, the city itself, or the patron saint of housework, Decimus could not guess.

He found Domitia already at her work. She stood over a tub the size of a cattle trough, hands sunk to the wrist in a froth thick enough to support small wildlife. Her sleeves were rolled, her hair bound tight, and her eyes fixed on the task with the single-mindedness of the professionally disappointed.

He paused in the threshold, feeling immediately out of place. His toga, though no longer crisp with blood, had acquired new stains in the morning's work. The heat made him itch, and he was aware, as never before, of how poorly he matched the clarity of purpose on display.

Domitia did not look up. "You're late," she said, not as accusation but as confirmation of a fact already entered in the ledger.

"I had to rewrite the past," he said. "It took longer than expected."

She snorted, a sound efficiently delivered. "I would offer you a seat, but there's nowhere left in Rome that's clean."

He stepped forward, feet sticking with each motion, and produced, from inside his cloak, a knife. He set it on the table with a delicacy usually reserved for glassware or unexploded ordinance.

She eyed it, then resumed her scrubbing. "Is that the best you could do?"

"I didn't think you'd want it back blunt."

A smile flickered at the corner of her mouth, then vanished beneath the steam.

He watched her work, the rhythmic up-and-down, the methodical torment of linen and silk. "You lost a lot yesterday," he said.

She shrugged, never breaking cadence. "We all did."

A silence followed, thick enough to stir with a stick.

She dipped a tunic into the tub, the water darkening to a hue somewhere between regret and resignation. "Do you know what they say about the city's memory?"

"That it never improves with age."

She nodded. "Or with rewrites."

He rested his elbows on the battered table. The knife

glinted, out of place among the soap and lime. "What will you do now?" he asked.

She wrung out the tunic with the efficiency of a man strangling a chicken. "Same as always. I'll wash away what I can. Stains are mostly about surface tension, you know. If you keep at it long enough, even blood comes out."

He stared at his hands, unsure whether the residue there was ink, sweat, or something less forgivable. "And if it doesn't?"

She threw the tunic into a basket, picked up another, and said, "Then you call it a new fashion. Or you wait until everyone else is stained the same, and call it tradition."

He managed a laugh, brittle at the edges.

Domitia's movements slowed. She reached for a cloth, handed it to him. "Here. For the hands." She did not specify whether she meant the stains of yesterday, or those of today.

He took it. The rag was rough, but not unkind. He wiped at his knuckles, watched the new brown smear the old. "Are you angry?" he said, without looking up.

She paused, as if consulting the room's many echoes. "No. It's not a useful feeling. The city doesn't care, so why should I?"

He placed the cloth back on the table. "Somebody has to."

She made no reply.

They stood for a moment in the rising heat, the water in the tubs churning, the effigy in the corner flickering as if it too had something to say but preferred to remain out of it.

He moved to leave. She stopped him with a word.

"Flaccus."

He turned.

"When they put up the statue," she said, "make sure they get the cheekbones right."

He smiled. "It's already in the draft."

She resumed her scrubbing. "You always were a fast writer."

He left, the steam following him up the steps, the smell of lye etched into his clothes and, he suspected, into the lines of his hands.

Above, the city was brighter now, the morning still in progress. The sun glinted off the rooftops, highlighting the smoke rising from the Office of Official Histories and the distant shimmer of the forum, where men were already arguing over what had happened, and what it meant.

Decimus found a bench in the shade and sat, watching the world unfold in its new, imperfect version.

He thought, for a moment, about statues and cheekbones, about laundry and knives, and about the stories that would outlive all of them.

He knew, as Domitia did, that the stains would never truly come out. But he also knew that, in time, even the worst of them faded to a memory.

He opened his satchel, took out his pen, and began to write.

History, he thought, could wait for its revision. For now, there was a city to remember, and a day to survive.

TWENTY-THREE

The Senate's temporary dais had been raised, in a fit of optimism, just high enough that those on it could avoid the reach of thrown fruit, but not so high as to suggest elitism. It was flanked, on either side, by laurel wreaths so heavily perfumed that they threatened to induce a mass fainting, and by an honour guard of togaed dignitaries, each studiously avoiding eye contact with the others. At the top, centre stage, Decimus Flaccus stood with the Official Account of the Assassination of Gaius Julius Caesar rolled under his arm, and the knowledge that he was about to read a text with more versions in circulation than the Sibylline Books.

Below him, the crowd swelled. Some had come to mourn, as evidenced by the black sashes, streaming eyes, and the practiced ululation of the city's professional keeners. Most had come to be seen mourning, and had stationed themselves with calculated proximity to both the portable public fountains and the men selling limited-edition "He Came, He Saw, He Conquered" sandals.

Still others, with the genetic memory of Rome's last seventeen public executions, anticipated either violence or, at the very least, commemorative sausage.

A band of children made a circuit of the assembly, their faces painted with the names of famous generals, their hands clutching baskets of knock-off laurel crowns. Someone had already managed to drop an amphora of commemorative wine, and the resulting puddle was being briskly mopped by a woman who, by her apron and expression, intended to bottle the runoff and sell it as a collector's item before the day was out.

Decimus drew a breath, unrolled the scroll, and let the first sentence ring out:

"On the morning of the Ides, the sun shone full on Rome, as if to witness the greatest sacrifice since the days of our forebears..."

He let the words settle. The crowd, practiced in the rhythms of civic lament, responded with a murmur just short of applause. Behind him, a row of bronze-faced bureaucrats leaned in synchrony to stamp each paragraph with the city's official seal as he read it, a process so literal that one, whose job it was to emboss the word "VALOUR" onto the account, did so at the very instant Decimus uttered it.

He continued, voice level, but with the faintest edge of disbelief audible to anyone who knew him:

"—betrayed by those he trusted, felled not in battle, but by the blackest envy of his own Senate—"

A gasp, perfectly timed, emanated from the front row, where Senator Fabius, now self-appointed custodian of public emotion, bowed his head with such gravity that his neck seemed to shorten. The audience responded with scattered sobbing, and, from the back, a shout of, "It's always the good ones!" followed by, "Except last time!"

Decimus skipped two lines, as had been rehearsed, to avoid the passage that might have implied fault on the part of the city's hiring policies.

"And yet, though his blood anointed the Forum stones—"

At this, the crowd's response was unexpectedly vigorous: a roar, rising, then a flurry of raised hands. Decimus glanced up, uncertain whether he had triggered a riot. He saw, on the left flank, a butcher distributing, at a markup, loaves of bread spattered with "authentic Caesar blood" (dyed beetroot, or perhaps not), which explained both the uproar and the sudden line forming at his stall.

He returned to the script, suppressing a smile.

"—from that noble sacrifice, the Republic is reborn, strengthened, and prepared to carry forth the vision of its greatest son..."

On cue, Fabius dabbed at his eyes with a monogrammed cloth. A mother in the second rank pinched her child, who obligingly began to wail. The rest of the dignitaries maintained their expressions: equal parts consternation, hunger, and the sort of resignation found in the less ambitious statues of the Forum.

Decimus scanned the crowd. He located Lucilla Minor at the rear, her height and bearing unmistakable even in civilian dress. She wore the toga of official mourning, but her arms were folded so tight across her chest that her hands had gone white. Her expression, rigid, managed to convey both contempt and pity, aimed, in alternating waves, at the dais and at the citizenry before it. She caught Decimus's eye. For a moment, he thought she would give him a sign—some signal of solidarity or disdain—but instead, she turned, her back to the stage, and left before the reading reached its halfway point.

He felt the loss of her gaze like a dropped stitch.

The remainder of the Account was a monument to compromise, every clause weighed and triple-checked, every metaphor subjected to committee. He recited the portion about Caesar's "immortal vision" with such mechanical precision that even the stampers behind him began to lose interest, their seals coming down with a lag, or, in one case, so far off the mark that it landed on a note pad rather than the actual scroll.

The final lines, honed to a sheen by the Office's new subcommittee on Civil Unity, ran thus:

"Though his body is gone, his spirit remains—unbreakable, indomitable, and fixed forever in the soul of Rome. Let us mark this day not as a defeat, but as a renewal, a testament to the power of our shared destiny."

He let the scroll close with a thump, and stepped back. Applause followed, ragged but adequate. The band of children began a chant, which failed to catch on but succeeded in providing a rhythmic backdrop for the dispersal of the dignitaries.

Fabius, ever the opportunist, strode to Decimus and, projecting his voice for the benefit of any still paying attention, said, "Bravely done, Flaccus. The Senate will not forget your loyalty."

Decimus bowed, just enough to register, and replied, "I can only hope it will remember this day for what it is."

Fabius gave a searching look, as if unsure whether to be complimented or insulted, then decided on neither and moved on to his next audience.

The bureaucrats gathered up the scroll, now spattered with both official seals and the odd flake of laurel. One of them, an apprentice with more ink on his tunic than in his inkwell, lingered. He offered Decimus a blank sheet and said, "If you wish to add a personal note for the annals, sir, now is the time. They say the Dictator's soul is still unsettled."

Decimus took the sheet, folded it in half, and, for reasons he could not articulate, wrote on it: *History is not what happened. It's what survives the edits.*

He handed it back. The apprentice read the line, smiled in the sly way of those who recognised code, and tucked it among the day's receipts.

The crowd, now loosened by the conclusion, began to move off in search of food or further spectacle. Decimus watched them go. He noticed, at the perimeter, two boys hawking palm-sized busts of the deceased—each one painted with a fresh wound on the cheek, and a removable laurel for "hours of fun, now with improved stabbing action."

He scanned the dispersal for Lucilla, but she was gone, as if she had never been there at all.

The dais was already being dismantled by a pair of city contractors, who handled the structure with the care of men certain it would be needed again within the month. The laurel wreaths, now wilting, were being divested of their best leaves by opportunists. A woman nearby attempted to barter a bag of the stuff to a passing priest, who declined with the explanation that, after this morning, "the gods had indigestion."

A figure approached from the side: Senator Cassianus, a man who had once written a treatise on the proper sequence of public mourning and now specialised in the aftermath. He drew up beside Decimus and murmured, "Fine performance. Tell me—was any of it true?"

Decimus replied, "True enough for the purpose."

Cassianus smiled, lips barely parting. "I thought so. The part about the comet was particularly moving."

"They always appreciate a comet," said Decimus. "It absolves the living."

Cassianus considered this, then took his leave, vanishing into a cluster of functionaries debating whether tomorrow's commemorative festival would require a re-drafting of the narrative, or merely a change in footwear.

As Decimus prepared to follow the crowd, he felt a tug at his sleeve. He looked down to see a girl, perhaps seven, holding up a scrap of parchment. On it, in the wobbling script of the half-literate, was written:

"New Caesar Coming Soon?"

He regarded the question, then the child, who waited with the patience of one certain she would get an answer.

He shrugged, and said, "Best to watch the sky."

The girl nodded, satisfied, and rejoined her peers, who were now auditioning for the role of mob in tomor-row's pageant.

Decimus descended from the dais, his legs stiffer than

he remembered. The city had already resumed its ordinary business, the interlude of sorrow now just one more layer of background noise. He walked through the thinning crowd, ignoring the shouts of the vendors and the hollow wail of the keeners, until he reached the shadowed portico of the Office of Official Histories.

The new office was as much an accident as a reward. Decimus Flaccus had not asked for a private chamber, but then, he supposed, neither had Caesar asked for a knife in the ribs, and both had come about through an identical process of slow, inexorable delegation. The renovations had proceeded with the urgency of a city eager to forget, which was to say: fresh plaster on the walls, new brass lock on the door, and—most astonishingly—three matched oil lamps mounted above the desk, their glass chimneys shining with imported clarity.

He sat behind a desk that was not only polished, but waxed with the sort of attention to detail that implied a future inspection. Through the triple-arched window, the Temple of Concord stood illuminated in white torchlight, the nighttime city reduced to its barest bones of order and aspiration.

Scrolls had colonised every available surface. The day's quota alone overflowed the trays: there were requests for republication ("Truth in Short Form," "History for Schools"), follow-up queries from the Ministry of Moral Memory, and, most recently, a thick bundle marked "URGENT: Temple Revisions." The latter comprised five competing poetic adaptations of Caesar's last words, each more elaborate than the last, and all of them demonstrably false.

In the corner, next to the stove, sat the "TRUTH?" pile. It had grown smaller since the first week, not because the contents were being processed, but because every few days a cleaner came by and quietly relocated the more dangerous files to the basement archive. Decimus had not objected. He had learned, in his first week on the job, that some stories were best left in the dark, and that the city's appetite for myth far outpaced its taste for accuracy.

He took up his quill and reviewed the topmost scroll, a request for a school edition of the Ides. The note in the margin read: "Please adjust for under-twelves—less gore, more optimism." He considered, then under-lined the phrase "sacrifice for the common good" and removed the detail about the self-wringing intestines. The next scroll requested a "Hymn to the Fallen Leader," to be sung in alternating stanzas by the city's schoolchildren and its livestock handlers. He pencilled in a suggestion: "Add stanza on posthumous clemency for minor offences."

A rap sounded on the door, hesitant but persistent. He looked up to see a courier—one of the newer hires, face unmarked by cynicism and still hopeful for a future not spent in archives—bowing slightly, a fresh sheaf of blank scrolls cradled in his arms.

"Delivery for the Office of Official Histories," the boy announced, as if the room might have failed to notice.

Decimus gestured to the inbox. "Just there, please. Try not to disturb the existing stratigraphy."

The boy placed the scrolls with care, then lingered, as if the act of witnessing the inner sanctum might itself be educational.

"Will there be a new decree about the Ides?" the courier asked. "My family says there's to be a different version every month."

Decimus considered. "That's the plan."

The boy grinned. "Better than taxes, sir."

Decimus returned the smile, which was only slightly forced. "Depends on who's collecting."

The boy departed. Decimus returned to his work, but now found the rhythm interrupted. The lamplight, once steady, now flickered with the breeze that crept in through an unseen crack. He thought of the crowd outside the Curia that morning, the sound of their cheers and their indifference blending into one indistinguishable hum. The Official Account had gone over well, he supposed; the crowd had eaten it as they ate everything else.

He wondered, for the first time in a while, if it mattered that the scroll was true.

Evening advanced. The city's soundtrack faded to the soft percussion of sandals on wet flagstone and the intermittent yowl of a cat displeased with the state of the Republic.

He considered the day, the ceremony, the butcher's bread, the child's question, Lucilla's absence. He thought about the city's memory, and about the version of history that would last longest.

He put pen to parchment and, without pausing, wrote:

"*And so, on the Ides of March, Julius Caesar fell—heroically, nobly, and very much on schedule. Please see appendix III for approved phrasing.*"

He smiled, thin and crooked. The lamp's light caught the words, illuminating them for a moment before they merged with the rest of the city's stories, archived and unread.

He capped the ink. He waited for the page to dry.

Outside, the Temple of Concord glowed, indifferent and eternal.

Inside, Decimus wrote on.

TWENTY-FOUR

Rome, having survived itself yet again, resumed its customary activities with the professional briskness of a city that believed only in the future, and only as an excuse for lunch. The evidence of recent crisis had been tidied away: banners from the last parade were now tablecloths in the Subura's second-rate taverns, and the blood stains in the Curia had been overpainted with a hue so optimistic that senators now complained of glare.

In the temple district, Licinia presided over a congregation of twelve. The official number was closer to three, but, through the subtle magic of distributed seating and the occasional hired statue, the room pulsed with the illusion of critical mass. The annex itself, leased from a defunct cult of barley-worshippers, had been retrofitted for the Bacchic revival by removing all furniture above the height of a knee. Wine splashed in communal bowls, from which the faithful (or merely thirsty) drew their libations. At the front, Licinia, hair wild, gestured with the deliberate amplitude of a woman who believed in her own volume.

"Let the new omens be poured!" she cried, upending a pitcher over a tray of goblets. The resulting puddle spread with satisfying velocity across the altar, displacing two votive candles and what might once have been a sacrificial muffin. "Drink and forget! Or, failing that, remember in the correct order!"

The cultists echoed her, some with real conviction, others with the blank cheer of a man humiliated in every other sphere.

Licinia grinned, teeth stained with either ink or second-press Malvasia.

Across town, Tribune Scaevola laboured in exile. His new office, inherited from a retired notary, was less a chamber than a storage opportunity, its walls lined with the doomed ambitions of prior occupants. Scaevola hunched over the latest law code, methodically inserting pages of handwritten "supplements" into the gaps between sections. Each supplement contained, in code and footnote, the evidence that might someday reconstitute the day's true events.

He paused only to sharpen his stylus and, once every hour, to recite a line from the preamble to the Republic's founding charter. "We are not governed by fate, but by the laws we make for ourselves," he muttered, and wondered, not for the first time, who had last rewritten that section.

At the laundry, Domitia ruled over her domain with a confidence never fully acknowledged by the city's official record. The steam, the clatter of paddles, the perpetual scent of lye and lemon peel: these were her elements, and she moved among them as a conductor among her instruments. On the benches, piles of folded toga gleamed white as threat. She eyed the workers, who scrubbed with the silent efficiency of the truly motivated.

But the true business was elsewhere. On a side table, concealed beneath a blanket of drying undergarments, a series of wrapped bundles changed hands with the regularity of a city bus. The runners who collected them never lingered, and Domitia never spoke their names. She managed the operation with flicks of the wrist, nods, and, when required, the raised eyebrow of doom.

In the afternoon, Lucilla Minor could be found at her desk in the Curia's north annex. The chamber, once a repository for ceremonial scrolls, now served as the war-room for Rome's next crisis, which was always at least half-invented. Lucilla, ever precise, had already drafted the first three pages of a treatise titled "Senatus Confuse-dus," a detailed analysis of the present mess, its causes, and the several possible futures.

She wrote in neat, stabbing characters, her pen stabbing at the page as if to intimidate it into compliance. Between paragraphs, she looked up at the window, as if to confirm that the world still existed, then resumed writing. She kept, on the corner of her desk, a bronze bust of Minerva; today, she had blindfolded the statue, on the principle that the goddess of wisdom deserved a break.

At the city's best-kept tavern, Hortensius enjoyed his retirement. He had, through an admixture of luck and deep understanding of the betting markets, managed to parlay a minor pension into a series of profitable side wagers. The current pool centred on the fate of the donkey: would the animal achieve official recognition, or be quietly sent to the sausage plant? Hortensius, always a contrarian, had placed his money on "canonisation," and now collected his winnings with the delight of a man who had spent a lifetime losing lesser bets.

As dusk bled into the city, public events resumed. The main square hosted a statue-unveiling, as the Curia's newest marble was revealed with a flourish and, in a break from tradition, only a modest riot. The statue itself was not of Caesar, nor of any living official, but a stylised laurel wreath, its base inscribed: "To All Who Serve, And All Who Are Served." An official, chosen for his ability to read aloud without error, intoned the dedication. The crowd, never much moved by stone, clapped politely and dispersed.

Elsewhere, the Offices of Official Histories held a ribbon-cutting to celebrate their new "Truth Suite"—a suite of three rooms, each devoted to a different interpretation of current events. In the first, the junior scribes practised their prose. In the second, the censors wielded red pens with gleeful abandon, their goal to "shorten the public memory to manageable length." In the third, a fresh batch of "prophecy vendors" rehearsed tomorrow's omens, all to be distributed via the new official notice-board: one at every corner, with each household receiving a government-mandated two omens per day.

The city's prophets, denied their freelance trade, staged a protest in front of the Temple of Mercury. They wore sandwich boards: "Will Foretell for Food" and "Omens Not Approved by the State Still Valid."

Passersby, having seen worse, ignored them. A child bought a prediction for a sesterce; the prophet, an old woman with the lungs of a balladeer, shouted, "Tomorrow will be much like today, but stranger." The child nodded, satisfied.

Night fell as it always did, without permission. In the emptying streets, a hush returned, and in the gaps between houses, the old, slow wind resumed its journey from the river to the hill.

On the steps of the Capitol, the donkey stood alone. The animal's coat had been scrubbed to a near-mirror finish, and a garland of laurel had been draped around its neck, though the donkey had already begun to consume it with the slow, considered appetite of the truly wise. Behind the animal, a small bronze plaque had been affixed to the marble.

It read:

IN HONOUR OF ALL WHO WITNESSED

The donkey chewed, then paused to regard the city below: its lights, its noises, its insatiable hunger for new stories. For a moment, it seemed the animal might bray, might offer a statement or a verdict. Instead, it lowered its head, nibbled the last of the leaves, and let history, such as it was, continue on.

In the distance, a band played a tune for the next parade, already slightly off-key.

The record, as always, stood open to revision.

***

Read the next book in the Imperium, Interrupted Series: *Legion of the Damned*.

RECEIVE YOUR FREE NOVELLA

www.jonsmith.net

MAILING LIST

Want to receive advance information about future publications?

Fancy exclusive access to freebies, special offers and bonus material?

Feel that your life isn't complete without Jon's monthly musings about writing, reading and publishing?

There's a solution! Sign up today to Jon's mailing list:

https://jonsmith.net/mailing-list

NOTE FROM THE AUTHOR

Hi,

Thanks so much for reading *Et Tu, Brute*!

It was a lot of fun to write. I truly hope it was an entertaining read.

If you enjoyed the book, I would be incredibly grateful if you'd be so kind as to leave a review.

Reviews really help authors for a number of reasons, not least, providing feedback on what readers like and improving visibility of the book on online retail sites.

Thanks in advance and I look forward to reading your thoughts.

Jon

BINGE THE SERIES

ABOUT THE AUTHOR

Jon Smith is the bestselling author of more than 50 books for children, teens, and adults. His books have sold over half a million copies and have been published in seven languages.

In addition to writing books, Jon is an award-winning screenwriter and musical theatre lyricist and librettist with productions at the Birmingham Hippodrome, Belfast Waterfront, London's Park Theatre and PJPAC, Kuala Lumpur.

A father of four, he lives near Liverpool with his wife and their two school-age children.

When he grows up he'd like to be a librarian.

www.jonsmith.net

X x.com/jonsmith_author

instagram.com/jonsmith_author

goodreads.com/jonsmith_author

amazon.com/author/jonsmith

facebook.com/authorjonsmith